The doorbell rang. Yanking open the door, Laura was surprised to see Paul. She searched her mind for why he would show up on a Saturday morning. "Hi," she said.

"Morning." He extended a basket of muffins. "Fresh from the bakery."

Muffins? From Paul Russell, who'd barely acknowledged her presence in his office for the past week? "Oh... How nice," she said. "Well, then, come in."

He entered, his steps tentative.

"I'll get some coffee." She led him to the kitchen, then prepared the coffee and put the muffins on a plate. "You're out and about early," she said. It was the closest her manners would allow her to come to asking why he was here.

"I realized I hadn't properly welcomed you and the kids," he said.

That was one way to put it, she thought. He had all but put the brakes on the welcoming committee and steered it out of town. But now, it seemed, Paul Russell might be changing his tune.

Books by Bonnie K. Winn

Love Inspired

A Family All Her Own #158
Family Ties #186
Promise of Grace #222
Protected Hearts #299
Child of Mine #348
To Love Again #395

BONNIE K. WINN

is a hopeless romantic who's written incessantly since the third grade. So it seemed only natural that she turned to romance writing. A seasoned author of historical and contemporary romance, Bonnie has won numerous awards for her bestselling books. *Affaire de Coeur* chose her as one of the Top Ten Romance Writers in America.

Bonnie loves writing contemporary romance because she can set her stories in the modern cities close to her heart and explore the endlessly fascinating strengths of today's woman.

Living in the foothills of the Rockies gives her plenty of inspiration and a touch of whimsy, as well. She shares her life with her husband, son and a spunky Westie terrier who lends his characteristics to many pets in her stories. Bonnie's keeping mum about anyone else's characteristics she may have borrowed.

To Love Again
Bonnie K. Winn

Steeple Hill®

Published by Steeple Hill Books™

STEEPLE HILL BOOKS

Steeple
Hill®

ISBN-13: 978-0-373-81309-4
ISBN-10:   0-373-81309-0

TO LOVE AGAIN

www.SteepleHill.com

Printed in U.S.A.

And Ruth said, Entreat me not to leave thee,
or to return from following after thee:
for whither thou goest, I will go; and where thou
lodgest, I will lodge: thy people shall be
my people, and thy God my God.

—*Ruth* 1:16

To Karen Elizabeth Rigley, sister and friend.
For all you do. For all you are.

Prologue

Houston, Texas

Laura Manning dreaded what was coming. The reading of her husband's will. But, as she'd been doing for the past fourteen years, she carried out her prescribed role. She greeted Jerry's family as they arrived, settling them into the leather chairs and couch in her late husband's study, making certain they were at ease, refilling coffee cups. Jerry only had a few cousins, and his grandparents had long since passed away. He hadn't been close to any of his relatives, but his cousins had been named in his will.

Hushed voices from the hall signaled more arrivals.

"Hello, Edward, Meredith." Laura hugged her father-in-law, and accepted the brush of her mother-in-law's cheek that passed as a lukewarm greeting.

"Sorry we're late," Edward began.

"We can't be expected to run on a timetable." Meredith gripped a lace handkerchief, already crumpled. "I've just lost my only child!"

Edward's eyes met Laura's, then he glanced away.

Meredith looked around the spacious, circular entry. "Where are the children?"

"At the neighbor's." Laura straightened a calla lily on the round table that anchored the room. "They're not old enough for this."

"Kirsten's thirteen," Meredith objected.

Laura winced. She really didn't want to further upset her mother-in-law. "I don't think that's old enough. Everyone else is in the study if you want to join them."

Meredith dabbed at her eyes. "They can hardly begin without us." She tottered in as though about to collapse, taking the chair closest to the desk while Edward sat in one of the two seats together Laura had reserved for them.

She poured coffee for them both.

Her friend, Donna, offered her a steadying arm when she stumbled and it looked as if she might spill the pot. Grateful for her presence, her only ally in the room, Laura squeezed her hand.

The doorbell rang. She was only expecting one other person, Jerry's business partner, Paul Russell. Although she didn't know him well, she hoped he'd be another friendly face in the room.

Opening the door, she was struck again by the tall, engaging man's appearance. Thick dark hair, on the long side. Equally dark eyes and a strong jaw.

"It's good to see you," she greeted him.

Something she couldn't decipher flickered in his somber expression, then disappeared. "You, too."

Because of the occasion, she wasn't put off by his reticence. "Come in to Jerry's study—everyone's gathered there. Can I get you some coffee?"

He followed, his footfalls crisp against the marble floor. "No, thank you."

Jerry's lawyer, Daryl McGrath, a man Laura had met only once before, sat at her late husband's desk. A stream of sunshine lit the room, edging past the heavy linen drapes she had pushed open that morning.

After she and Paul took the last chairs, McGrath began to read aloud from the long, ponderous document. Jerry couldn't have made his will short and simple. He had to have his final moment. It wasn't a kind thought. But Jerry had stolen most of her kind thoughts over the years. It was hard to believe she had once loved him more than life. Handsome, charming, he had overwhelmed her with attention and affection. And she had been so desperate to be loved, to escape her scarred home life. But she hadn't really known him. And the abuse he had dished out later, once they were married, had all but killed her.

Fingering the very proper pearls at her neck, Laura wanted to shrink into the straight-backed chair, out of sight of Jerry's family. Instead, she crossed her legs, straightening her slim-skirted black dress over her sheer, dark hose. She hoped that her clothes, along with her dark hair, might help her blend into the dark wood.

She listened to the small bequests to Jerry's favorite male cousins, a gold watch, an expensive money clip. When McGrath read the next bequest, Laura frowned. Jerry had given several pieces of furniture, including the baby grand piano, to his parents.

If it hadn't been for the children's piano lessons, she wouldn't have cared. Material things had never been high on her list of priorities. She would have been happy in a tiny house with the barest necessities if Jerry had been the kind, considerate man she had once believed him to be.

Holding her hands in her lap, Laura fingered her wedding band.

"Now we come to the major bequests," McGrath announced. "The primary residence, business interests, the cash and insurance." He rustled several papers. "Jerry thought out his final wishes very carefully. He wanted to provide for his family in all aspects."

Premonition washed over her, and Laura straightened in her chair.

"To that end," McGrath continued, "he appointed Paul Russell as his executor and trustee."

Sitting perfectly still, she could barely breathe.

"Jerry left his entire estate, in trust, to be divided equally, between his children, Kirsten Elaine Manning and Gregory Gerard Manning…. I'm afraid there's no provision for you, Mrs. Manning."

No provision. Despite her shock, Laura knew what that meant. It was fancy legal talk for what her shaking insides were trying to absorb. Jerry still had a choke hold on her and he wasn't going to let go.

Chapter One

"I'm terribly sorry, Mrs. Manning, but I'm afraid there's little you can do, other than bring an action against the trust." Tom Baldwin, the lawyer Laura had contacted, looked at her kindly, his sympathetic tone releasing the tears that lurked close to the surface.

"Sue my own children?" Laura reached for a tissue. "That's not an option."

"Perhaps the executor will be open to your plans."

Laura grasped her purse, needing to cling to something, anything. The world had turned on end since the reading of the will and she wasn't sure what was real anymore. Most of their acquaintances assumed Jerry's death would have affected her this way. But they didn't know him like she did. To them he was the engaging charmer, the great, outgoing guy who'd been a football star in high school and college. And she'd been the shy loner he'd chosen to marry. Few had understood the match, but plenty of girls had envied her. Because Jerry was "the man."

Jerry's only stroke of bad luck was colon cancer, undetected until it was too late. But he had enough time to dictate the terms of his will. Six weeks from diagnosis to death.

She had wondered if the diagnosis would change him, but not even a death sentence could reverse whatever propelled his meanness. For her, his death couldn't negate fourteen years of emotional abuse, of being worn down, of always being afraid that his temper would blow. And he'd seen to it that she had to ask Paul, a virtual stranger, permission for nearly everything.

"Mrs. Manning?" Baldwin's quiet voice prodded her.

"I'm sorry." She wiped her eyes. "I have no idea how the executor will feel."

Baldwin frowned. "Really? Wasn't he your husband's partner?"

"Yes. But I only met him a few times."

"How extraordinary."

"Not if you had known Jerry. He didn't include me in anything related to the business. All I really know about Paul is that he was Jerry's college friend and that he lives in a small town in the hill country."

And two days earlier, as soon as the will had been

read, Paul had left, telling her to talk to Jerry's lawyer about her concerns. He'd mentioned something about a sick sister and apologized to the Mannings for his abrupt departure.

"You and Jerry didn't go to college together?"

"No, I'm four years younger. I met him when I was a high school senior." She'd been too young and gullible, anxious to get away from her equally abusive parents. Trapped in the cycle of demoralizing emotional abuse. Why her? "Anyway, Jerry and Paul go way back."

"But you had no idea that Jerry had given him such extensive control?"

"No." She stared at the framed law degrees on the wall, not reading them. "He told me he'd had a new will drawn up because of the complexities of the business."

Baldwin peered at the thick sheaf of papers. "He's left Russell in charge of everything from determining the amount of your allowance to where your children can attend school."

She leaned forward, her knees pressing the desk. "Can I fight that?"

"Yes. But I warn you, it will be expensive."

And where would she get the money?

"Surely half the house is mine because of community property?"

Baldwin nodded. "Yes. But unless you can buy

out your children's half, you can't sell it. Any of the assets you wish to claim, remember, will necessitate litigation. And again, that will be expensive."

Her throat closed. For fourteen years Jerry had bullied her, had killed almost everything that she was. And he was still doing it from the grave.

Tom Baldwin wasn't an unfeeling man. "Talk to Paul Russell," he urged. "Surely he'll see that this document was drawn up in haste, by a man who wasn't seeing clearly. Death makes people do crazy things."

Not in this case. This move was one hundred percent pure Jerry.

Rosewood, Texas

Paul jogged the remaining three blocks of his run, slowing as he came to Main Street. He turned at Borbey House, inhaling the smell of pies baking in Annie Warren's kitchen. He groaned. The Sorenson bakery was in the next block. They were probably baking cinnamon buns. It was what he deserved for putting his office right smack in the middle of them both.

His cell phone rang. Since it was still early, he considered ignoring it as he decided between pie and pastry, but by habit he flipped open the phone, slowing to a walk.

"Russell."

It took him a few moments to realize who was calling and why. As he did, his mood soured. "Laura, slow down. It's clear to me from Jerry's will that he didn't act in haste, that he knew exactly what he wanted."

Her voice was plaintive. "What about what I want for my children?"

"I don't mean any disrespect, but my friend chose me to be his executor and I have to act on his behalf." *My friend who's now gone.* Leaving a gaping hole in both the business and what had been an eighteen-year friendship. Jerry had been like an older brother, first taking him under his wing at the University of Texas.

Jerry hadn't treated him like the small town hick some others had, instead drawing him into his group of friends. Grateful, Paul had been eager to go into partnership with him after graduation. It seemed hard to believe he had been such a vital, strong man only a short time ago.

"What about the company?" she was asking.

He stopped walking, bending at the waist to stretch. "What about it?"

"Jerry was your partner. I'm prepared to take his place."

"Excuse me?" Paul was glad she couldn't see his face.

"I said I'm prepared to take his place."

"You want to work in the firm?" He wiped the sweat from his neck.

"Yes."

Paul stretched his right leg. "I don't remember Jerry ever talking about you helping with the deals."

"Well…I didn't exactly. That doesn't mean I can't learn."

"And who's supposed to teach you?"

"You. I know I don't have my agent's license yet, but I can take classes toward that. It's the investment part of the business I need to learn and there's not a school for that."

"You want me to teach you?" He switched legs, stretching the left. "That's not a good idea."

"But—"

"I'm sure you mean well, but it would be more helpful to all concerned if you concentrate on raising your kids." He started walking, anxious to end the call. Jerry hadn't said anything, but Paul suspected his friend must have had reason to worry about Laura to have left him as executor instead of his wife. He had promised Jerry he would watch out for the children. Jerry hadn't asked the same for Laura.

"That's not what I want."

"And Jerry didn't want to die young, but we don't all get what we want." He exhaled, trying not to be harsh with her. "Sorry to rush, but I'm on my way to the office. Bye." Not waiting for a reply, he clicked off. His appetite ruined, he jogged the rest of the way to his office, waving to Ethan Warren who was climbing into his car, no doubt on his way to the school.

The phone was ringing as Paul entered. Turning on the lights, he crossed to the desk that faced the entrance. Breathless, he grabbed the phone. "Distinctive Properties."

"I wasn't finished."

It was her.

"Paul, like it or not, we're stuck with each other because of Jerry's will. I want to work in the company. It was half Jerry's, so why shouldn't I?"

Paul glanced around his small office, imagining sharing any part of it. Since he contracted out the majority of his work, he'd never needed a large space for employees. And he'd always been partial to the Victorian building. He kept the furnishings spare—one extra desk, two chairs, a few lamps. He considered it more important for the office to fit his work instead of making it a showplace. "Your allowance is reasonable. You don't need to work. A lot of women would be happy not to leave their kids to go to a job."

"I want…I…" Her voice trailed off.

Listening, he heard muffled sounds. "Mrs. Manning? Laura? Are you there?"

It took a moment. "Yes."

"You don't even know what you're asking to get into. This is a tough industry. Flipping property is even worse than selling homes—you know, traditional real estate. Buying investment houses, then renovating on a tight schedule and reselling them to make a quick profit is like chasing sharks. It only sounds like fun." She didn't laugh. That didn't surprise him. He had never heard her laugh, she had looked unhappy every time he'd ever seen her. "It's stressful and risky, you have to know what you're doing all the time. If you mess up, you not only lose your own shirt, but your investors', as well. It's not the place for the weakhearted. I know you've had a lot to take in lately." He eased into his well-used wooden chair and put his feet up on the scarred desk. "Maybe I was too abrupt with you earlier. But, this isn't something you want to do. Trust me. You're going to have your hands full with the kids, keeping up with your house."

"You don't understand—"

"What's to understand? Jerry just died. You're confused."

"I'm *not* confused."

Paul rubbed his eyes. "Laura, maybe you can talk to a therapist or—"

"I don't need a therapist."

His other line rang. "I'm sorry but I have to take another call."

He had always understood the initial attraction Jerry must have felt for her. Tall, slim, glossy dark hair, haunting green eyes. But she always acted downtrodden. He likened her to a whipped dog. And he never could figure out why. Jerry was a great guy and treated her like a queen. But then some women, like his ex-fiancée, only thought about money. Maybe Jerry's beautiful home wasn't as big as she wanted. Maybe she wanted one in the exclusive River Oaks area of town where the millionaires lived.

And personality wasn't the only thing she lacked. Her husband had just died and she hadn't expressed a shred of grief.

Laura stumbled outside, needing the open air. Even the muggy air the recent rain had rendered. When Paul Russell had pushed, she hadn't been able to summon the courage to push back, to find the words to explain how much she needed her freedom. She couldn't bear to be under Jerry's thumb another moment.

How was she going to convince him to let her learn the trade? Clearly not over the phone. She would have to talk to him in person, argue her case.

"Mom?" Kirsten sounded annoyed as she came outside to join her on the deck.

"I'm here."

"It's like a zillion degrees out here and the humidity's killing my hair," Kirsten complained.

"Did you need something?"

Kirsten frowned. "I'm going to stay at Nana's for the weekend."

No asking permission, not even the consideration that she might need to. This had to stop. Laura had tried so hard to keep Jerry's abuse hidden from the children that she had become a doormat in her daughter's eyes. And it was becoming more blatant since Jerry's death.

"I don't think so, Kirsten."

Her daughter stomped her foot and Laura noticed she was wearing a new pair of shoes, another present from her grandmother. "But Nana said we were going shopping!"

"You didn't ask me for permission."

Kirsten scowled, her pert features so much like her father's. "What's the big deal?"

Maybe it had been a mistake to try to keep Jerry's image untarnished, to keep their arguing secret. "I'm your mother, Kirsten. Without my permission, you don't go anywhere. And that includes your grandparents'."

"That's not fair!"

"Those are the rules. You wouldn't have thought you could go without permission when your father was alive."

Kirsten was definitely her daddy's girl. She shook the blond hair—exactly like his—blue duplicates of her father's eyes now furious. "Daddy would have said yes!"

"Maybe. And maybe you'll think twice next time about *announcing* you've got plans, instead of asking for permission."

"Nana's right. We should come live with her."

Laura stared at her. "What?"

"Nana says you won't be able to manage and we should come live with her. I think she's right. And Gregg will think she's right, too, when I tell him."

Fear unsettled her. Up until now, Gregg hadn't acted like his older sister. But if Kirsten tried to influence him... And Meredith...if she was campaigning to take the children away...

Laura had to do something. Living only two blocks away from her in-laws, it would be easy for Kirsten to visit them as often as she wished. Yet moving was nearly impossible. She couldn't sell the house. And if she leased it out...she didn't want to move her children into an area that wasn't safe just to find lower rent. And that was the only way she could imagine finding the funds to go back to school herself. Unless...

Unless she learned the basics of flipping houses from Paul Russell. She hadn't been able to find her courage in years, but now...now she had to.

* * *

Laura fretted and agonized for days. If she stayed in Houston, her life would be out of her control as it had been during her marriage. But, if she could convince Paul Russell… She knew she didn't have any practical experience to bring to the table, but… She moved away from the window, her steps hesitant, and reached for the phone.

She dialed Donna's number. They'd been friends since the third grade, and Donna was the only person she had confided in throughout her marriage. Donna answered on the third ring.

"I'm glad you're home."

"I was checking out what's left in my fridge. Pretty pathetic."

Laura frowned. Donna was a software engineer and she worked out of her home office. "You must be busy."

"Just finished a deadline."

"Oh." Laura hesitated. Donna was always rushed after a deadline, playing catch up.

"What's going on?"

Laura explained.

"I can take the kids to school, pick them up," Donna offered. "And I'll stay until you get home."

"Are you sure it's not an inconvenience?"

"I'll bring my laptop, start on my new project. Besides, you probably have food in your fridge."

Laura let out a breath. "What would I do without you?"

Donna laughed. "Let's not find out. And stop worrying. Things will work out."

Early the following morning, before traffic could clog the roads, Laura set out for Rosewood. Although both freeways heading west out of the city were always packed, Laura's predawn head start helped.

It was nearly ten o'clock when she arrived. She hadn't known what to expect, but the charm of the perfectly kept Victorian buildings surprised her. Equally old elm trees shaded the wide sidewalks. No boarded-up buildings on Main Street. Looked like the town was alive and kicking. She spotted an old-fashioned drugstore that made her think of the one her grandmother used to take her to for ice-cream sodas when she was a little girl. It was one of the few positive memories from her childhood.

Intrigued, Laura slowed down, savoring a place that hadn't been edged out by a superstore or run down by neglect. She spotted cheery gingham curtains in the café windows and smiled. She needed cheer more than breakfast, which she had skipped in her hurry to get an early start, but she didn't want to stop. She wanted to catch Paul early.

She found his office easily enough. The simple brass plaque above the wide black awning announced Distinctive Properties, Ltd.

Grasping the brass door handle, she tried to take hold of her courage as easily. She stepped inside. Paul sat at an old mahogany desk facing the entrance. A second, similar desk was angled next to his, but it was empty. The office was small, with some leather chairs, filing cabinets, coffee-maker and not much else. There was another door at the rear.

Looking back at Paul, she remembered to smile. But her courage failed her when he scowled.

Then she realized he was on the phone. Two actually. At least he was holding two. One was a cell. It rang as she watched.

Deftly he put the first call on hold, answered the second, then switched back to the first. A moment later he finally noticed her.

Her first impression hadn't been that far off. He looked annoyed as he ended both calls.

"Good morning." She tried to sound confident, but her voice came out sounding more like a frightened bird.

"Hello," he said cautiously. "This is a surprise."

"I suppose it is." *Courage. Keep your courage.* "I came to talk to you about the company."

"We already talked about it."

"No." She bit her lip. "You brushed me off."

His phone rang. "You want to talk *now?*"

"Yes, please."

"You couldn't have picked a worse time. I'm speaking to investors."

Her anxiety heightened. "In an hour then?"

"It's Monday morning. I'm calling my most important contacts." He scrunched his mouth in contemplation. "I could hook up with you, say, late this afternoon."

"This *afternoon?*"

He reached for the phone. "If you really want to talk. If not—"

"No! I mean yes. I want to talk." She calculated quickly. Donna said she would stay as long as necessary. "So, this afternoon?"

"Okay."

Laura picked up a card from his desk and scribbled her cell phone number on it. "Call me when you're free?"

"Fine." His phone rang again.

Awkwardly, she stepped back. "I'll see myself out then."

He was already absorbed in the phone conversation.

Out on the sidewalk, she breathed in the clean spring air, the smell of baking bread laced with blooming hyacinths. Unexpectedly, her stomach rumbled. In spite of nerves.

She glanced down the street. A sign in the next block caught her eye. Borbey House Bed and

Breakfast. She didn't know just how long Paul Russell planned to put her off, but she intended to stick around until he spoke to her, even if that meant staying until the following day. It might be smart to book a room, just in case. Besides, she was tired. It had taken everything she had to screw up her courage for this visit. She hated this weakness in herself. Before she had married, she wouldn't have been so intimidated, so frightened. *This was just a negotiation.* With Jerry's best friend. Why couldn't Jerry have let her go? She hadn't wanted him to get sick, to die.... But she had thought at last she would be out from under his control.

She pulled out her cell phone.

Donna answered on the second ring, and Laura explained the situation.

"Stay as long as you need. My work's coming along fine. You know I love borrowing other people's children."

Laura hesitated, unaccustomed to asking favors. "It could be longer than just overnight."

"Stay as long as you need."

Laura clutched the phone. "I can't tell you how much I appreciate this."

"Hey, what are friends for?"

Laura felt a little better as she walked the short distance to Borbey House. A bell tinkled when she pushed open the door to the bed-and-breakfast and stepped into an immaculate front room, furnished with inviting antique couches.

"Be right there," a woman called.

Laura waited by an ancient breakfront that looked like the sign-in desk. Within moments, a perky, attractive woman who looked to be about her age, scooted into the room. "Hi!" She wiped her hands on her apron. "Just finishing up in the kitchen. How can I help you?"

"I'm hoping you have a room for tonight. Well, maybe longer. I'm not sure exactly how long I'll be here." The way she felt right now she could climb into bed and pull the covers over her head.

"I have one that fronts on Main Street if you like the view or one that looks out on the back garden if you'd prefer complete quiet. You can see both, if you'd like, and then choose." Dark eyes twinkled as the woman pushed her brown hair behind her ear.

"That's a tough call, but I think I'll take the quiet." She needed it to recoup.

"Fine. If you change your mind, just let me know. It's no trouble switching you around." Laura signed the guest book, a simple register, her writing shaky. "I'm Annie Warren and this is my place, mine and my husband's."

"Glad to meet you." She reached for her purse, fumbling with her wallet. "You'll need my credit card."

Annie waved her hands. "Not necessary. We can do that when you check out."

Laura stared, amazed.

Annie laughed. "I doubt you want to get up at four in the morning to skip out. Besides, a little trust goes a long way."

"That's a kind, if somewhat precarious, way to live in this world."

"It works for me."

Laura's anxiety eased somewhat.

"Have you had your breakfast?" Annie put her hands on her narrow hips.

"Actually no. But if it's too late—"

"Nope. I was just getting around to mine. Would you like to join me?"

Laura was touched by the offer. "I'd love to."

"The dining room's still set for breakfast. I haven't cleared the buffet. The warmers are on under the bacon and sausage, the eggs, too. The griddle's hot and I was about to make pancakes. Or whatever you like."

"I adore pancakes. I didn't expect such bounty." Laura wandered over to the antique buffet. Jams— she'd guess homemade—in crystal dishes begged to be spread on the plump rolls. And there was a basket of sticky buns as well. She felt as though she'd stepped back into another time when people lingered over breakfast.

"I just made some fresh coffee." Annie indicated from the stove. "And there's orange juice on the buffet."

"Let me," Laura offered. "What do you take in your coffee?"

"Thanks." Annie pointed. " Just a little cream."

Laura poured them each a coffee. Retrieving the pitcher of orange juice, she carried it to the only table with place settings.

Annie followed shortly with a platter of fluffy pancakes. "This time of year we get a lot of tourists because of the wildflowers, but it's still mostly weekends right now."

"I'm not here for flowers." She stopped. She didn't intend to tell this stranger anything about why she was here. Annie just smiled.

"Rosewood's a good place to be."

"Oh?"

"People are welcoming here."

Laura reached for the syrup. "I'm just here for a visit."

"It's a fine place to visit, too."

"Is the real estate market doing well here?"

Annie poured some cream into her mug. "I don't really know. But you could check with Paul Russell down the street."

Laura choked on her bite of pancake.

As she coughed, Annie patted her on the back and

handed her a glass of water. "Sip slowly. The maple syrup *is* strong. I should have warned you."

Once she caught her breath, Laura said. "No, it's lovely, really." She sipped more water, took some time wiping her mouth with the cotton napkin. "Is he a friend of yours?"

"Paul? Yes. He's a member of my church."

"Church?" Laura didn't mean to spit the word, but Jerry hadn't included church in their plans. He'd been too busy with barbecues, boating and golf. And between the disillusion with her marriage and the control Jerry held over her, she had drifted far from the days when her grandmother had taken her to church.

Annie must have sensed her discomfort. "How about some orange juice?"

"Thank you."

Annie poured her a glass. "So, are you here to check out the real estate market?"

"In a way," Laura hedged. She had been hiding the truth about her abusive marriage for so long it was second nature to keep everything quiet.

"I have a friend, Emma McAllister, whose husband is a contractor. He's working on a house not far from here. He just built a new home for the owner." She put the pitcher down. "And they don't want to sell this one because they want to keep it in the family. Seth's fixing it up to rent it. If you want to look inside, he's probably around."

"Oh, I don't know...."

"I hope I'm not being pushy. It's become a habit since I started running the bed-and-breakfast. That, and because I was single so long and rattled around the house alone I tend to treat my guests as friends." Annie grinned. "Sorry, there I go. But the house really is great—if you want to get an idea of the market here."

"I could take down the directions, I suppose." She did have hours to kill and maybe she would show Paul she had initiative and could learn quickly.

"If Seth's not there, check the back door. It might be unlocked," Annie said, getting up to find a pen and paper.

"Really? The house is left open?"

"This is Rosewood. We don't have any crime to speak of."

But leave an empty house unlocked? Laura couldn't imagine such a thing. She had lived in the city so long, in the *right* area, the one Jerry had chosen. Still, security systems were a fact of life.

Intrigued, after breakfast Laura followed the directions Annie had given her. She found the address easily. And sighed as she stared at the two-story folk Victorian, falling immediately in love with the front gable and side wings, corbels, the gothic details, the welcoming porch. The rosebushes that appeared to be as old as the house itself.

A man was sweeping up on the driveway.

"Hi. Are you Seth?"

"No. The boss isn't here."

"Oh. I heard I might be able to take a quick look inside."

He paused, holding the broom still. "Sure. The owners are planning to put it up for rent. I imagine they want people to look at it. The front door's unlocked."

"Thanks." She entered the foyer, then stepped into a large living room with high ceilings and a beautiful fireplace with an intricately carved mantel. Plaster walls, original woodwork, tall arched windows that allowed the light to stream in. It was amazing. The rest of the rooms were just as great. She wasn't in real estate yet, but this place would have to rent for a small fortune. Well, some lucky family would be happy here.

She checked her watch. Even dawdling, she still had way too much time to kill. She thought about going back to the bed-and-breakfast for a nap, but she didn't want to wake up disoriented for the meeting. So she decided to check out the town.

The entire place was a step back in time. She wandered around Whitaker Woods, a store full of handmade furniture, each piece a one-of-a-kind design. She peeked into the windows of the costume shop, Try It On, intrigued by the unique designs she hadn't expected to find in such a small town.

Her phone rang. "Hello."

"Laura? Paul Russell. I can't squeeze in a meeting after all." He sounded tense.

"Oh." She looked down the street at *Distinctive Properties*. It was within walking distance.

Before she lost her courage, she headed for his office. "I only need a minute."

"Another time."

Paul was still on the phone when she pushed open the door. She took the chair angled in front of his desk.

"I told you I didn't have time to meet," he said after he hung up.

"That's why I came to you." She gripped her purse.

He frowned. "You just show up here, after I told you I'm too busy?"

Every nerve she possessed crowded into her throat. "We need to talk."

"I told you. Flipping property isn't easy. You have to be able to hold steady when you've bought a property, poured a ton of renovation money into it. Navigating between investors and sellers… It takes commitment, guts." He held up his hands as though to say he knew she didn't have either.

"I have both," she lied. If she'd had any real

courage, she would have left Jerry years ago. But she couldn't tell Paul that.

"And it takes expertise."

Laura leaned forward. "Which you can teach me."

"I've already told you—"

"Please don't reject this out of hand." Laura bit her lip, wondering how much of the truth she should tell him, guessing he wouldn't believe much. "I know you think you owe it to Jerry to run the firm as you see fit, but don't you owe it to him to listen to me, as well? To consider what I can offer? Half the profits will benefit his children."

She wasn't convincing him. She could see that.

"You're forgetting a pretty important technicality."

She blinked in confusion.

"Even if I agreed to teach you, you live in Houston."

"But you and Jerry made that work."

"Because Jerry knew what he was doing. He acquired properties in the Houston area, supervised those renovations. I locate the investors, make sure the money's in place. And I buy homes in this area for flipping, as well. I can't teach you how to find and then buy the right properties, not from here."

She opened her mouth, but no sound emerged. Her grip on the purse tightened. *Not from here.* Unless she did something more drastic than she had planned. Fortunately, she'd had an idea.

Chapter Two

Two days later Laura arrived back in Houston, flushed with anticipation and fear. She had rented the incredible house on Elm Street in Rosewood. To her amazement, it had been surprisingly affordable, far below what she would have had to pay in Houston for something a fraction as nice. Now she had to lease out her own home and tell the children...and her in-laws. At the thought, she nearly turned the car around in the opposite direction. But it had to be done.

"Okay, guys, we need to talk," she said to the kids as soon as she let herself in. "No, stay—please," she added to Donna. "I need your support."

Donna settled back down on the sofa, turning off the TV. Laura had already phoned her on the return trip, cluing her in on her unexpected plans.

Kirsten sighed as she collapsed into the cavernous chair that had been her father's favorite. Again it struck Laura how much her daughter resembled him.

Gregg snuggled next to Laura, still young enough to be excited by his mother's return. She smoothed the dark hair on his forehead. He had always taken after her in more than just appearance. They shared the same temperament.

"Since your father died, a lot of things have changed. And we have to make a new life for ourselves. For that to happen, I need to learn about your dad's work. And the only way I can learn is for us to move to where his partner lives."

"Move?" Kirsten jumped up, all her casual disdain gone. "We can't move. All my friends are here."

"You'll make new friends—"

"I don't want new friends." Kirsten's voice was shrill. "Nana and Grandpa won't let you do this."

Laura knew her declaration of independence wouldn't be met with enthusiasm. She also knew that she would have to stick firm, not show her fear. "It's not their decision. You'll be able to visit them, but we have to stick together as a family, make this work for all of us."

"Moving to some hick town won't work!" Tears streamed down Kirsten's face.

Laura got up to comfort her daughter, but Kirsten backed away. "You can't make me go!" She galloped up the stairs, slamming her door behind her. The sound echoed through the quiet house.

Donna's expression was sympathetic, but Laura's heart sank. She looked down at her son. "What about you, pal?"

Gregg hunched his skinny shoulders. "S'okay, I guess. Do I still get to play peewee ball?"

She hugged him. Hard. "I'm sure you will. Rosewood has the very best stuff for kids. It's one of the things that decided me. It's really safe—kids ride their bikes to school and their moms don't worry. And they have all kinds of great things for you to do."

He screwed his face into lines of thought. "Where are we going to live?"

Laura described the house, the nearby park. "And your room has a killer view of the whole street."

"Cool."

She hugged him again, wishing the transition could be as easy for her daughter. But Kirsten would have to adjust. They all would.

Gregg wriggled free. "I'm gonna go start packing."

"Okay, sweetie. We'll get some boxes later today. Maybe just go through your toys for a start. See if there are some you'd like to put in the donation box."

After he had trooped upstairs, Donna whistled. "This is fast, Laura."

"I know. And I didn't plan on it. To be honest,

when the idea hit me, I was scared to death. Then I found out that I could afford this great house—oh, Donna, you'll love it. And the town is safe, the kind of place you want to raise kids in. And I liked the people, well, Annie and Ethan Warren, the ones who run the bed-and-breakfast. He's a schoolteacher, and she runs the inn." Laura paused for breath. "You know how bad it's been—how terrible things were with Jerry. Now I've got another chance..." She stood, pacing toward the large window that looked out on the fashionable street. "Does that sound as awful out loud as when I think it?"

"Not for anyone who really knew Jerry. I don't know how you stuck it out this long with him. If he hadn't gotten sick...Well, I know you wouldn't have wished that for him, but I don't think you'd have escaped any other way." Donna hesitated. "I'm guessing Kirsten's reaction will seem mild compared to her grandparents'."

Laura sat down, then glanced toward the staircase. "I imagine she's already on the phone, telling her grandmother." She leaned her head back on the top of the sofa, picturing how furious they would be. Hit hard by the loss of their son, they drifted between grief and anger.

"They can't keep you here," Donna said wistfully.

"I'm going to miss you. But it's not that far. You can visit—bring your laptop. You'll like Rosewood,

I know it. And the house has an extra bedroom with your name on it."

"I *am* mobile," Donna admitted.

Laura smiled. "I don't know what I would have done without you all these years. With Jerry..."

"You don't have to say it. I know. Maybe you're right. Rosewood's atmosphere might be great for my work."

"Not to mention there could be new single men for you to meet."

Donna laughed. "If I can't find the right one in a city of more than four million, what chance do I have in a teeny town?"

"Different priorities?"

"Does that mean you've spotted someone there?" Donna looked intrigued. "Paul Russell?"

Laura shook her head. "Hardly. Not only am I a brand-new widow...but Paul? He can barely stand to speak to me. I'm not sure why, either. He seemed to have made his mind up about me before he ever met me."

"Something Jerry said?"

Laura thought of Paul's disapproving expression. "Maybe. But I don't think Jerry would have said anything negative. You know how he was about appearances."

"Maybe Paul's just an odd duck, then."

"Maybe." But Laura hadn't thought so. Well,

until he had been so set against her joining the firm. "Donna, will you stay for dinner? My in-laws will probably make an appearance and I need the moral support."

"Sure. I'm a glutton for punishment." Donna rose, picking up glasses as she walked toward the kitchen.

"Thanks. You're a lifesaver."

"I put some chicken out to thaw. How 'bout if I work on dinner while you take a few minutes for yourself—maybe grab a shower."

"You sure you don't mind?"

"It's fun for me to cook for more than one."

Grateful, Laura hugged her friend. "I won't be long."

"Take as long as you want."

Upstairs, Laura shed her traveling clothes and luxuriated in a long, hot shower. She washed her hair, willing the pounding water to erase her worries. Pulling on a thick, ankle-length terry robe, she combed her hair. Donna was right. A hot shower had been just what she needed.

Humming, she skipped down the stairs, pausing at the landing that curved down to the final four steps. Her in-laws stood in the foyer. Donna, clearly uncomfortable, glanced up at her.

Wishing she'd taken the time to get dressed, Laura knotted the sash to her robe. She felt vulnerable, at a disadvantage. "Hello, Edward, Meredith."

Her father-in-law managed a small smile, but Meredith began crying.

Laura felt the pit of her stomach drop. "Let's go into the living room."

Trailing them, Laura knew she had to get this over with, but it didn't lessen her trepidation. She'd always wanted a closer relationship with her in-laws, but Edward traveled so much for work and Meredith had never encouraged a deeper connection. Despite the fact that they had never been close, she had always hoped Meredith would become a true mother figure, especially since she really didn't have one of her own. But the woman was entrenched in a social life that hadn't included her daughter-in-law. Laura knew they both thought Jerry had married beneath himself.

Meredith had barely taken a seat when she began her tirade, waving her lace handkerchief like a flag. "Laura, what are you thinking?"

Laura started to answer. "I—"

"You're not thinking of the children, just yourself. Jerry did everything he could to keep this family together." She sniffed into the rumpled square of cotton. "Now, the moment he's gone, you want to rip it to pieces."

Laura hated conflict, but she didn't have any choice. Again, she wished she and Meredith had the sort of relationship that encouraged confidences. She would like to pour out the whole story—tell her about the real Jerry, who emerged behind closed doors. But what purpose could it serve now? To hurt his parents, turn them against her? Their only child, they had idolized him. "You don't understand, Meredith. I'm doing what I think is best for my family."

"By taking them from their home, everything they know? From us? Hardly, Laura. You're being selfish."

The words hurt. "I'm sorry you feel that way, but I have to do what I believe is right. And Rosewood's not that far. You can visit—"

Edward leaned forward. "Laura, why don't you consider taking up something to get your mind off Jerry's passing? You could go to school or…"

With what? Her allowance was too small for that. "I appreciate the suggestion, Edward. But we need a new start. And we can't get it here." Laura caught sight of Kirsten hovering in the doorway.

"You seem to have forgotten that the children are part of *our* family, too." Meredith's thin lips tightened.

Laura hated this tension. It seemed her entire life had been nothing but fighting. She wanted so much for it to stop. "And the kids can visit you."

"I want to stay here with them!" Kirsten nearly shrieked the words.

Meredith held her arms out to her granddaughter and Kirsten rushed into them. "See what you're doing to her!"

"She'll adjust. It won't be easy. I know that." She reached for her courage. "But my mind's made up."

"Then expect a fight, my dear." Meredith rubbed Kirsten's back. "This isn't over."

The hard knot in Laura's stomach grew even harder. Why couldn't her in-laws see that she was fighting to save her family? That she wished she didn't have to uproot them? But they hadn't seen anything wrong in the way their son had dictated his will, easily accepting Paul as the executor.

In the end, there wasn't anything Meredith could do about the children.

Laura contacted a Realtor who was thrilled to get a listing in the exclusive area and immediately leased out her home to an executive and his family. She committed the house for a year. By then she would know if she could succeed or if she would have to come back.

Without the funds for professional movers, Laura had to downscale. Calling it an estate rather than a garage sale, she culled through the pieces. Even with the rent from the house, it would be tight at first. Kirsten was horrified and locked herself in her room, but Gregg helped her tag the furniture.

Laura hadn't planned on selling any of the children's things anyway, not that she could get her daughter to listen. She thought of the baby grand piano and the other pieces Jerry had given to his parents. She certainly could have used the money.

Laura pitched some of Jerry's shirts in a box for the Salvation Army. They'd collected a lot of things over the duration of their marriage, but Laura wasn't attached to them. If it hadn't been for the kids, she would have liked to forget all of that time. So most of the art and collectibles were going on the block, as well. They had been Jerry's taste anyway, too contemporary for the turn-of-the-century house they were moving to.

Once the plans were in motion, Laura lost no time having the sale, then packing up the house. She hired the cheapest movers she could find.

Farewells with Meredith and Edward were filled with tears and hugs for the children. They were stiff with her, showing their displeasure. Kirsten huffed as she got in the car, her entire face a pout. Despite her own uncertainty, Laura didn't cave. Instead she headed west out of the city. This time her anticipation edged ahead of her fear.

"This old house?" Kirsten asked in disgust when they pulled into the driveway.

Laura hung on to her patience. It had been a long drive, which her daughter had made feel even longer by sulking the entire way. It was also late in the day and they were all tired.

"Cool roof," Gregg offered, bouncing out of the car. "Big, old yard! Are there swings?"

Grateful for her youngest's attitude, Laura followed. She had barely turned the key in the lock when she spotted the moving truck arriving.

Soon the driver and his helper were unloading the furniture.

"Excuse me, some of these cartons should be upstairs," Laura said, when they'd finished taking the beds and chests up.

"Not in the contract," one of the men replied as he deposited her kitchen table in the middle of the living room.

Laura sighed. She *had* chosen the cheapest movers she could find. She and the kids could carry the boxes upstairs. Since she had packed them herself she hadn't collected big ones anyway. "All right. Could you assemble the beds next? That way I can get them ready before…"

The man was shaking his head. "Not in the contract."

Laura gaped at him. She couldn't help it.

The man shrugged and headed back to the truck.

Maybe she should have paid just a little more.

"Mom!" Gregg ran inside. "There's a lady here."

Laura poked her head around the kitchen door. Annie had been trying to follow Gregg, but he was already hopping back through the maze of boxes to watch the movers.

"I'm here."

"Hi! I just saw the truck. Welcome!"

"Thanks."

Annie looked around at the haphazard cartons. "Wow."

Laura hated to admit again how blunder-headed she was. "I picked a discount moving company," she finally said.

"Ah. Well, I love a bargain. It's like finding treasure."

Laura straightened a box that was tilted precariously to one side. "I'm afraid it's going to take a complete treasure hunt to find anything here."

"That's not something you have to worry about tonight. You'll be my guests."

She didn't have the money for rooms at the bed-and-breakfast. "I hadn't planned—"

Annie dodged to one side as the movers carried in a chest of drawers. "As my *guests*. Ethan and I insist. It's our welcome gift to you and the children."

"We can't—"

"Yes, you can. I know the argument. The bed-and-breakfast is a business. But it's not our only income. Remember, Ethan is a teacher. And we *know* where our sheets and towels are," she added with a laugh.

"That does sound like heaven." The kids would

be exhausted by the time the movers left. And the thought of Annie's inviting beds… "But isn't this your busy season, with the wildflowers?"

"It's Thursday. My weekenders don't start checking in until tomorrow."

"Well…"

"And you'll have dinner with us."

Laura opened her mouth to protest, but Annie waved her off. "What? You'll take the kids for burgers instead? I don't think so."

Laura was so grateful for her kindness, she felt the sting of tears.

Annie gave her a reassuring hug. "You're home now. And that's what friends are for."

It had been so long since Laura had been able to let friends into her life. She hadn't been able to confide the terrible state of her marriage to anyone other than Donna. She had been too ashamed. Instinctively Jerry hadn't liked Donna, so she hadn't been comfortable coming around when he was home. Swallowing, Laura nodded. "Thank you."

"You're welcome. We'll see you when you're done here."

Kirsten stood at the bottom of the stairs as Annie introduced herself on the way out. "I'll see you and your family for dinner later, Kirsten."

"Okay." She looked back at her mother.

"She invited us to spend the night at her bed-and-breakfast. We get to sleep on beds that are already put together."

Kirsten didn't look impressed.

It took another hour for the movers to unload the rest of their things. By then Laura was exhausted and ready to round up the kids.

Annie and Ethan were so welcoming that even Kirsten was subdued. They led the family back to the large kitchen rather than the dining room.

"It's where we eat," Annie explained. "We think it's cozier."

A pot of chicken and dumplings simmered on the stove and the big round table was set for five with dishes that looked as though they had been in the house since it was built.

Ethan, a cheerful, quick-witted man with a no-ticeable sense of fun, pulled out chairs for Laura and Kirsten. "And, you, young man, how about sitting next to me?"

Pleased to be singled out, Gregg hopped onto the spindle-back chair. "Okay."

After they were seated, Ethan and Annie bowed their heads. It took Laura a moment to react, then she gestured to her children to follow suit. Her throat tightened as she heard Ethan ask the Lord to watch over her and the children as they settled into their new home.

Then Annie began to dish up the fragrant stew

while Ethan questioned the kids about their schools in the city, explaining that he was a teacher.

"You have to make kids do homework and take tests?" Kirsten asked him with a hint of accusation.

"Yes, but I also direct plays, plan the field trips. Most of the kids love drama."

Kirsten sipped her milk, but didn't reply.

"Do you teach any other subjects?" Laura asked, sending Kirsten a reproving look.

"English. I try to make that fun for the kids, too. We act out Shakespeare—makes it easier for everyone to understand." He held out his bowl and Annie filled it with steaming chicken and dumplings. "I know it's not everybody's favorite, but I think most of us can get something out of his works."

"If they understand them?" Laura prompted.

"Exactly."

She looked down at her full bowl. "This smells delicious."

"My grandmother's recipe," Annie told her. "She and my grandfather raised me here."

Laura wondered about Annie's parents as she glanced at the old portraits on the walls. "It's a great house...better, it's a great home."

Annie grinned, meeting her husband's eyes. "Thank you."

He clasped her hand and lifted it to his lips. "My Annie has the touch."

Laura felt a spurt of envy. Maybe it was the exhaustion that was just now setting in, but she felt very close to the edge of tears.

Annie reached over and patted her arm. "It's a big adjustment moving to a strange town, even one as inviting as Rosewood."

"Yes," Laura said, her voice thick. She cleared her throat.

After smoothing the napkin in her lap, Annie picked up her spoon. "The chicken and dumplings are guaranteed to fix whatever ails you."

"Annie made apple and cherry pie," Ethan told the children, rubbing his hands together. "Which do you like?"

"Cherry," Gregg answered immediately.

Kirsten shrugged.

"You'll have to try both then." This engaging man seemed the perfect complement to his kind, energetic wife. "Laura, you picked a fine house."

"We like it." Kirsten glared at her, but Gregg just kept eating his dumplings. "Have you lived in Rosewood long?"

"Grew up here." Ethan chuckled. "Thought I might have to leave to find a wife, then I met Annie."

"Luckily for me," Annie murmured.

"And we decided we wanted to make her family home ours." Ethan added a few hefty spoonfuls of sugar to his tea.

Laura dipped her spoon into the gravylike broth. "Are your furnishings original?"

"Most of them. Annie can tell you which ones belonged to her grandparents."

Annie passed a small dish of pickles that appeared to be homemade. "I had to add more beds, a few other things—but most everything was here. I did some rearranging, too."

"It seems more like a family home than a bed-and-breakfast." It was something that had struck Laura immediately.

Annie beamed. "Super! That's exactly what I've tried to achieve."

Ethan winked at his wife. "And we hope to fill it with children in time."

Annie blushed, a pretty pinkening of her pale skin. Ethan put his hand over hers. Yes, they were a lovely couple. Laura swallowed her longing, her sense of regret. Why couldn't she have met a man like Ethan? But then, on the surface, Jerry had seemed perfect, too.

Ethan had a way with kids that even Kirsten had a hard time deflecting. After dinner, he herded them both into the parlor by the kitchen to play games while Annie took Laura upstairs to show her their accommodations. Their generosity was overwhelming.

And in the morning Annie insisted on feeding

them a hot breakfast before they took off to their own house. The kids dawdled but Laura was anxious to get started unpacking.

When she finally unlocked the door of her new home, it was daunting to see the mound of boxes. But she and the kids had been there less than an hour when she heard the doorbell.

"Mom!" Gregg hollered.

She set down the bed frame, still clueless how to put it together. "Coming." Walking down the stairs she could hear the buzz of voices. Had her son allowed strangers into the house?

She was relieved to recognize Annie among some other women. "Hi."

"Laura, I've rounded up recruits. Cindy, Leah, Katherine, Grace and Emma."

Laura's hand flew to her chest. "I don't know what to say."

Redheaded Cindy grinned. "*Hello* will do just fine. Then divvy us up however you want."

Overwhelmed, Laura wasn't at all certain how to ask them to help.

"I'm especially helpful in the kitchen," Katherine suggested. "If that would all right. I could start sorting dishes, pots and pans."

"Oh, yes," Laura replied, relieved.

"And I'm good at toting boxes," Grace added.

"They're labeled," Laura said. "With the rooms

they belong in. I'm afraid they're all in a huge pile right now, no rhyme or reason."

"I can help with the boxes," Emma pointed out. "Rhyme's my specialty."

"And I can help Katherine in the kitchen," Leah offered.

"So, I can be your helper," Cindy said. "What were you doing when we got here?"

"Trying to put together a bed," Laura confessed, holding up a tiny screwdriver, the only one she'd been able to find.

"Ah." Cindy fished in her pocket for her cell phone. "When all else fails…"

Annie took Laura by the elbow and guided her out to the front porch. "You okay?"

Laura shoved her hands in her pockets. "Yes. Why?"

"I want to help, but I don't want to pressure you."

"It's not that…it's…" Laura looked out at the quiet street, the old houses that spoke of generations of families living and loving in the same place. "I haven't been accustomed to anything like this…it will take some getting used to. But I like it."

"Whew." Annie let out her breath.

"Didn't you tell me this was going to be *your* busy day?"

"Yes, but not for a while. I have time to help." Together they headed into the house.

Even though Laura wasn't accustomed to the sound of women's voices around her, the occasional laughter, she found she liked it immensely. Like a piece that had been missing, the chatter and occasional laughter fit perfectly.

After about a half hour of progress, she heard the low rumble of a man's voice, accompanied by the tread of boots going up the stairs, then the distinct thud of tools.

Cindy popped her head into the kitchen where Laura was consulting on the placement of dishes. "We'll have the beds put together in a few minutes if you want to come up and tell us where to position them."

"What? How?"

"I called my husband, Flynn. I knew he'd make sure the beds were put together right. I'm pretty handy, but I'd hate to try assembling them and have somebody crash in the middle of the night."

Laura pushed the hair off her forehead. "That would have been an initiation to the new house."

"I like your spirit!"

That wasn't something Laura had heard very often. Encouraged, she headed upstairs with Cindy. In Gregg's room, Flynn, a lean, handsome man, had assembled the bed and was helping Gregg with his computer.

He grinned at her, and she immediately liked the tall man with the ready smile.

"Mom, Flynn makes software programs," Gregg announced.

"That's great, sweetie. Hello, and thank you for coming and doing this."

"Always glad to help new friends."

Together they quickly figured out where the beds in her bedroom and Gregg's should go. Kirsten's took longer.

"I don't like it there." Kirsten frowned as they pushed the bed beneath the wide window.

Laura sighed. They'd already moved the bed three times. "We're running out of places to put it. We can always rearrange later."

Kirsten's room had a dormer ceiling, resulting in angled walls. Although architecturally interesting, it made arranging furniture difficult.

Kirsten's face drooped. "It's a pokey room."

"You think so?" Cindy asked. "I guess I'm the weird one, then. This is my favorite room in the house. Before I got married, I lived in a Victorian quite a bit like this one. And it was the interesting rooms like this one that convinced me to live there. I can just picture willowy curtains—and this fabulous window seat, well…I always felt it was so private. I could curl up with a book or music and it was a secret nook, all mine."

Kirsten looked over at the window seat. "I guess so."

"I plan to make cushions for it when you decide on your color scheme," Laura added.

They repositioned the bed one last time and then started on the other pieces. It was especially helpful to have Flynn's brawn to move the furniture into place. The room looked pretty well put together when they were done. She had hoped by making the room special, it might help to break down Kirsten's defenses.

"What now?" Flynn asked.

"Aren't we keeping you from your work?"

Flynn grinned. "One of the bonuses of being boss."

"We need to make sure we have all the upstairs boxes actually upstairs," Cindy told him.

"Aye, aye." He smiled. "Boss at work, that is."

"Pooh." Cindy's red hair seemed to crackle in the outpouring of sunlight from the windows. "Don't let him fool you. He's hardly henpecked. Do you know where the boxes with the sheets are?"

Laura felt so inept. "Not really."

"Don't worry, I'll find them. I want to make sure Flynn finds all the boxes that need to come up anyway."

Shaking her head at the resourcefulness of these women, Laura headed back downstairs. At noon, the doorbell rang. Although Laura had forgotten to plan for lunch, the women hadn't. Someone had ordered sandwiches—made with homemade bread—from the café down the street, along with soup, salad and brownies.

Even Kirsten relaxed as everyone in the house stopped to eat. The women knew each other so well, by the time lunch was over, the place rang with their laughter.

Laura learned that Katherine was the pastor of the Community Church. She had married her husband, Michael, after moving to Rosewood. Cindy was her best friend and she had married Flynn after the death of her sister—then his wife and mother of his triplets.

Grace had survived a horrific car accident that required numerous surgeries. Which was how she had met her husband, Noah, the finest surgeon in the area. But then, Grace was biased.

Emma had come to Rosewood through the witness protection program. Fortunately, the man who was stalking her had been caught and now was in prison for life. Even more fortunately, she had met her husband in Rosewood—Seth, the man who had refurbished this house.

And Leah had come to Rosewood from Los Angeles, in search of her child, who had been abducted by his father as an infant. Now, she and her son were reunited, and she was married to the man who had loved the boy as his own. They were expecting another child in six months.

Laura wanted to confide her own past, but she couldn't. Everything she had ever confided to Jerry had been turned around on her, more ammunition for him to belittle her with. Besides, her situation was so humiliating. It seemed as if she'd been ashamed all her life. From childhood when she couldn't invite friends over because of her parents' fighting.

Cindy stood and stretched. "If I eat another brownie, I'm going to bust."

"Me, too." Katherine began gathering empty paper plates.

By the time evening rolled around, the breakfast table was in place in its nook, all the boxes that had been stacked there previously now distributed appropriately. All the bedrooms were set up, bed linens and blankets on each bed, and towels were stacked neatly in the bathroom. Dishes, glasses, and pots and pans were put away in the kitchen cabinets.

As the women prepared to leave, they gave Laura a hug, and again she felt close to tears. Ridiculous, she told herself. More emotional than she'd felt since the death of her husband, since finding out about her own untenable situation.

"Thank you all so much. I don't know what to say."

"We're glad we could be here for you," Katherine murmured.

Emma shifted her purse to her shoulder. "And I'm supposed to tell you that Annie's bringing dinner."

"But, she's already done so much—"

"Don't fight it," Leah advised, leaning over to whisper. "She's my best friend and a definite keeper."

As Laura closed the door behind them, she finally gave in to tears.

"Mom?" Kirsten's voice wavered behind her.

Laura quickly wiped her cheeks. "Yes, sweetie?"

Kirsten stared at her for a moment. "Gregg's hungry."

"Annie's bringing dinner over. Isn't that thoughtful?"

She shrugged. "Yeah, I guess."

But Laura had seen a crack in Kirsten's rocky facade. It was a start. Now she just had to work on Paul. And pretend she had the courage she had lost so long ago.

Chapter Three

"You *moved* here?" Astonished, Paul got up from behind his desk, staring at her. Only a nut would pack up her children and move to a strange town on a whim. "What did you do with your house? You didn't leave it empty, did you?"

"Of course n—"

"You know you're supposed to consult with me before you make these decisions. That's why Jerry left the plans in place—to protect you and the children." He perched on the edge of the desk. "What were you thinking? Just hire movers and... Hey! Where'd you get the money to move?"

"You told me you couldn't teach me how to flip houses since I was living in Houston, so that left me one option—to move here." She edged back in the chair. "I rented a house over on Elm Street that I can afford on my allowance, then went back to Houston and leased out the house. And I had an estate sale to raise the money for moving costs. That and I used a bargain mover."

He pictured her selling everything Jerry had accumulated over his lifetime and groaned. An estate sale? In the short time since he had seen her it had to be a giveaway sale. And no telling what kind of people she had rented the house to. But she had him there. He wasn't sure he could interfere with that decision. She *did* own half the house by Texas law. As a broker he knew that. And he had never imagined that she would twist his words to mean that she could be part of the business by moving here. But he didn't know how to undo what she had done, either.

She shifted, loosening her grip on the chair. "So, what do we do first?"

"First?"

"You know, to begin my training."

He hadn't even begun to wrap his mind around what she had done yet. "Would you like some coffee?"

"Oh, um, yes. Okay." She started to get up. "Where is it?"

"I'll get it." He needed a minute to think. He crossed the room, filling two mugs. "Cream or sugar?"

"Just cream, thanks."

He handed her one of the mugs. "So, Laura. This was a huge step."

She warmed her hands on the steaming mug. "It was. But it means a lot to me. I explained that before."

"Settling in is going to be a big adjustment."

"I thought so, too." She lifted her gaze, her green eyes entreating. "But Rosewood's a lot different than Houston."

"You form opinions pretty fast."

She wondered if he thought that was bad. "It's hard not to."

"You'll have to enroll the kids in their new schools."

She swallowed a sip of the hot brew. "Did that yesterday."

"Really?"

"I didn't want them to miss any more than necessary. It's difficult enough to settle in a new school without having them get behind."

"Don't you have to have records transferred or something?"

"I did that." She took another tentative sip.

He put his mug down on the desk. "Still, you're going to need time unpacking, settling in—"

"No." She ran her fingers over the handle of the mug. "I'm ready. That's done for the most part. There's always more to do, but it's livable."

He pictured the house in a jumble of boxes. But that was why Jerry had named him executor, to keep an eye on how she was caring for the kids. "Laura, this isn't a school."

"Excuse me?"

"It's an office."

Her expression faltered. "But you said—"

"That I couldn't train you if you lived in Houston. But I can't stop working and set up classes, either."

"Then what?"

She had gone from hopeful to desperate in the space of minutes. She wouldn't last. "Start by spending some time in the office, watching what I do."

"Oh." Deflated, she gripped her mug tighter, then nodded. "Okay."

She would get bored fast. Sitting at the desk next to his, listening to only his side of telephone conversations, trying to digest a lot of financial information she couldn't possibly understand. He'd give her a week at the most before she stopped coming around. She'd probably get bored with Rosewood almost as soon.

The phone rang. And her tutoring began.

"So, how was school?" Laura put a plate of oatmeal raisin cookies on the table. She had made arrangements with Paul to be home each day before the children got in from school. Since he looked relieved at the suggestion, she guessed he would have been just as happy if she had suggested a much earlier quitting time.

Gregg grabbed a cookie. "There's a kid in my class who can cross his eyes, hold his breath and wiggle his ears. All at once."

"Impressive." She tweaked the tip of his nose. "Do you like your teacher?"

"Yeah." He took a swallow of milk. "She said next Monday we can all bring a pet for show-and-tell."

"Oh." They didn't have a pet.

"It's okay, Mom. Even if we had the aquarium set up I couldn't take it to school."

He always rolled with the punches. She put another cookie on his plate.

"Kirsten, how about you?"

She shrugged. "It's a school."

"Did you meet anyone who could wiggle their ears?"

Her daughter sighed. "Mom."

Nothing so unsophisticated for her daughter. "Let me rephrase. Did you meet anyone you liked?"

Kirsten was quiet for a few moments. "Kinda."

"Does this person have a name?"

"Mandy. She's sort of new, too. She moved here at the first of the year and started with the other kids." Kirsten broke her cookie into smaller pieces. "People think she's neat, though."

"They'll think you are, too." Laura had never worried about Kirsten's popularity. Like Jerry she had always attracted followers. She smoothed her daughter's hair, but Kirsten jerked back. Laura kept her sigh to herself.

"If I could catch a frog, I could take that on Monday," Gregg deliberated.

Kirsten shuddered. "Gross."

Laura poured more milk into Gregg's glass. "What if I talk to the teacher? See if you could bring your butterfly collection instead?"

"That'd be cool. It'd be my dead pets."

"Double gross." Kirsten rolled her eyes.

The doorbell rang. "After you're finished with your snack, homework, guys."

Laura went and opened the door. It was Katherine and Cindy.

"I hope this isn't a bad time," Katherine began.

"No, not at all." She gestured to the living room. "Come in, sit down."

"We thought you might need a hand with the rest of the boxes." Cindy held up her cell phone. "The girls are keeping the time open if you agree."

Laura was touched by their offer. "I can't ask you to keep helping."

"You didn't." Katherine tucked her keys into her pocket. "Would it be all right for us to phone the others?"

Laura bit her lip. "If you're sure it won't be putting you out…"

"We're sure." Cindy started dialing almost before the words were out of her mouth.

As the kids shyly passed through and headed upstairs, Laura noticed that Gregg had piled a few extra cookies on top of his books. Oh well, looked like dinner might be late anyway.

It seemed only moments passed before the women began to assemble. And they brought chocolates, brownies and cookies with them. Annie carried in two of her signature pies.

"Chocolate and sugar for fuel," Emma explained. "Only the bare necessities."

Again, laughter filled the old house along with the treble of women's chatter as they went up and down the stairs, unloading boxes, finding places for most everything.

Grace smiled, a mixture of sweetness and mischief. "This way you'll have to stay in touch with us—if you want to find anything."

Laura imagined that wouldn't be a hardship. "I never expected this much…help."

"I came from the city, too. I wasn't used to how neighborly people here are. And I wasn't comfortable with it, at first." She raised her scarred hand. "But it wound up helping me heal…inside."

It seemed this woman could see right through her.

"Laura, would you rather have these in the dining room or living room?" Leah held out a pair of slender brass candlesticks, turning them so the afternoon sun hit the aged patina.

"Um…dining room, I think."

Katherine was right behind her with a doll older than Laura herself. "For display, I'm guessing?"

"Yes. She was my grandmother's."

Katherine ran her fingers gently over the faded porcelain face. "I love things with history and sentiment. My house looks like I put it together from a jumble sale." One hand flew to cover her mouth. "Not that yours does—just the opposite, you have really stylish furniture."

"It's not my style, though," Laura confessed, shrugging off the unintentional slight. "My husband was the contemporary fan. I prefer the furnishings at Annie's."

"Like Cindy and Flynn," Katherine mused. "She loves Victorian and he likes ultramodern. They compromised by turning her house into a children's refuge center. Still, it always takes me aback when I see how the new one's furnished."

"And Cindy doesn't mind?" Laura wouldn't have thought the independent woman would capitulate so completely.

"She's so nuts over Flynn she said she could live in a cave and be happy."

No. Cindy and Flynn weren't anything like she and Jerry had been.

Grace touched Laura's arm. "I hope we're not upsetting you, talking about spouses."

"No. It's okay."

"If it ever does, will you tell us?"

Laura knew it wouldn't be a worry. "Okay. If you'll agree to tell me something."

"Sure."

"How did you get comfortable with the neighborly help?"

Grinning, Grace clapped her hands. "It's a long, long story. Which I'll be glad to tell you when we meet for lunch."

Laura found herself smiling, as well. "Lunch?"

"As soon as we can set it up."

Her smile grew. Jerry had frowned on anything she had done that took her away from the house. It had been difficult even to schedule her volunteer work. He had given in on that only because his mother encouraged Laura's efforts. But even casual lunches with Donna used to set him off. Now, her sense of freedom soared.

Chapter Four

Paul continued deliberating about his decision to allow Laura into the office. She was clinging like glue. And carrying home books on finance to study. She was there early every day, leaving just in time to meet her children after school. She took copious notes and asked so many questions, he couldn't doubt her dedication. But he worried that she might be neglecting the kids for her tutoring. He needed another opinion, so he headed over to see his parents.

The tallest trees in Rosewood were in the yard of the Russell family home. At least Paul thought so. Ever since he was a kid and his father had pushed him in the tire swing beneath the widest oak, Paul had believed that particular tree had reached all the way to the sky. And in the dusk it still looked that way.

No one was in the house, but he knew where to look.

They sat out back on the porch that stretched from one end of the house to the other. Although he'd had new lighting installed, they hadn't turned it on. Instead, an oil lamp flickered on the table and he guessed they held hands as they sat side by side in the ancient swing.

As long as he could remember, once he and his younger brothers and sisters had been put to bed for the night, his parents would slip out back to sit together. He used to wonder what they would talk about in their hushed voices. There had been worry, which he'd instinctively shared. He'd known his mother was happy, though. They'd all been. Because his dad had come back from the war—albeit injured. But even though he'd just been a kid, Paul had known they were lucky. His dad was an Air Force pilot and most of them hadn't made it back from Vietnam.

When he saw his parents, he questioned whether a love like theirs was even possible nowadays. Take that unpredictable Laura Manning. Jerry had probably thought she was a sweet, caring girl when he married her. He couldn't imagine his friend marrying someone so set on the bottom line, her chin practically dragging the ground because she wanted more. Had she changed so much? Or had she just fooled him?

"Hello, honey," his mother, Elizabeth, greeted him.

"It's quiet out here. No rugrats visiting?" His nieces and nephews were the delight of everyone in the family.

"Not tonight. How about some tea?" She started to rise.

"I can get it."

"You sound tired, son." Charles was close to all the siblings, but he'd always been particularly attuned to him.

This was the place Paul could always bring his troubles, always find understanding. He had already told them about Laura when Jerry had passed away, his concern for their children and her abrupt arrival in Rosewood. "It's the Manning family. I'm worried about the kids. I hate to think about what kind of mess they must be living in."

Charles leaned forward. "Haven't you gone over there yet?"

"You think I should?"

"How else are you going to know exactly what the conditions are?"

Elizabeth patted his arm. "It may not be as bad as you're guessing."

"I'd like to think not, but Dad's right, I have to see for myself. I've been putting it off because I'm not real sure what I'm going to do when I come face-to-face with it."

"You'll work that out, son." Charles rubbed his chin. "Jerry put his trust in you with good reason."

"And you can count on us to help," his mother added. "Maybe the boy would like story time at the library. I could watch out for him then." Elizabeth's job as a part-time librarian had helped the family through lean times, and she had been able to adjust her schedule around the continuing surgeries Charles had to go through year after year.

"I'll see, Mom. Thanks."

"And you can bring both children here if you need to," his father offered.

"Thanks, Dad." He sipped his cool tea.

"How is she doing in the office?" Elizabeth asked, offering him a plate of chocolate chip cookies.

He took one. "She makes notes constantly, listens to every word."

Charles stretched out his stiff legs. "Sounds like she really wants to learn."

"For now." He dusted the crumbs off his pants.

"Why don't you give her an honest chance," Elizabeth suggested, offering her husband the plate.

Paul stood. "It's going to be a waste of time."

Elizabeth frowned. "You don't know that."

"It's not like you to prejudge people," Charles said evenly.

"I'm just remembering Jerry's instructions." He leaned against the porch rail. "He wanted me to keep a close eye on the kids. He was probably worried that she would go through the money so fast there wouldn't be enough left to educate the kids."

Charles rubbed his bad knee. "Does she strike you as that sort of woman?"

Paul put his foot on the lowest rail. "She seems really needy, unhappy. And Jerry gave her a beautiful home and everything she wanted."

"Maybe it just seemed that way on the surface." Elizabeth shifted in the swing.

Paul sipped his tea, remembering. "Some women only think about money."

"And some don't," Elizabeth reminded him. She had led a life of sacrifice for her family and he was ashamed that he needed the reminder.

"Your mother's right. See for yourself, son."

By Saturday morning, Laura was exasperated. The *training* was practically nonexistent. All she had done so far that week was listen to Paul's phone calls and trail him around the office. She suspected his plan was to bore her to death so she'd give up and go home. But this was her home now, more of one than she had ever had.

She heard a loud thud upstairs. Then the trill of squabbling voices. The kids were wound so tight they were practically jumping off the walls. She needed to find them another outlet besides school.

The doorbell rang. What now?

Yanking open the door she was startled to see Paul. "Hi."

"Morning." He extended a box. "Muffins, fresh from the bakery."

"Oh… How nice. Well, then, come in."

He entered, his steps tentative. His expression, as he took in the tidy living room, seemed incredulous. "It smells great in here. What is that?"

"Beeswax, lemon. From waxing the furniture. Not very exotic, I'm afraid. The kitchen's this way." She led the way to the rear of the house. "Would you like some coffee? To go with the muffins?"

"You have some made?"

She wondered why he was so astonished. "Yes." She stirred a teaspoon of sugar into his coffee and set the mug on the table. After taking dessert plates from the sideboard, she placed them on the table, as well. "You're out and about early." It was the closest her manners would allow her to come to asking what he was doing there.

"I realized I hadn't properly welcomed you and the kids."

That was one way to put it. "I'm sure they'll enjoy the muffins. It was thoughtful of you to bring them."

He sneaked a glance toward the stairs. "The house looks really…good."

"It's special, isn't it? I was amazed at how much

you get for the price here compared to Houston. Renting, I mean, because I can't buy. Well, you know that." The awkwardness was crushing. "Um, would you like to see the rest? The kids are straightening up their rooms, but they're not in too bad a shape."

"Yeah, that'd be great."

They toured the downstairs first. "I love all the detail work." She passed her fingers over the fluted column of the fireplace. "The windows and molding. Can you imagine how much it would cost to build something like this today?"

"Actually, yes." He wandered around the living room. "It's my business to know."

Mortified, she paused. She had momentarily forgotten their relationship. She must sound like a dope! "Of course." Wishing she had a hole to drop through, she led him up the stairs.

"Didn't you bring very much with you?" Paul asked, still looking around.

"Sure, why?"

He shrugged. "Oh, just meant that it looks like everything's unpacked already."

"I wanted to get things back to normal as soon as possible. It's a big change for the kids. I still plan to do window coverings, pillows and such, but they'll come in time." She knocked on one of the tall doors. "Gregg? We have company."

Her son whipped open the door, his face expectant.

s he stared at Paul. As she began the introductions, she was pleased to see that Gregg had made his bed.

"Paul brought muffins."

"Cool!"

"Great room," Paul told him.

"Thanks." He spun on his tennies. "I still need to set up my aquarium and get some fish, but that's on Mom's list."

Of course, children his age did tell everything. "I haven't found the local pet shop yet."

"I could show you where that is," Paul offered. "I imagine Gregg's missing having his fish."

Laura gritted her teeth. It was a sensitive subject. She had persuaded her son that giving his fish to his best friend was a generous thing to do. Replacing them was going to be a special project for the two of them.

"Could we, Mom?" Gregg pleaded.

"We can go today if you have time." Paul thumbed through one of the books on the shelf.

"Please," her son continued.

How could she refuse? "Yes, we can go, Gregg."

Kirsten wasn't as thrilled. She was polite through the introductions until she heard the proposed destination. "The pet shop? Mother, why do we have to go there? *I'm* not six!"

"That will be enough, Kirsten. We're going to the pet shop."

Her resident pout returned.

Laura hid her frustration as she smiled at Paul. "We should all be ready in a few minutes."

"A few minutes!" Kirsten wailed.

Although her daughter's whine could have peeled the paint off the walls, Laura maintained her smile. "Yes, in a few minutes. It's a pet shop, not a coronation."

She wasn't sure why Paul had turned up today, but if he wanted to spend time with the children, he was going to see them warts and all.

Chapter Five

"The angel fish is pretty cool," Gregg decided as he watched the elegant creature glide gracefully through the water.

Paul spotted a sign atop the tank. The fish was one of a mated pair and he doubted Laura wanted to care for the offspring. He pointed to an adjacent tank. "How about these little ones?"

Gregg shrugged. "Guppies are okay I guess."

The boy knew his fish—this wasn't going to be as easy as he had imagined. It didn't help that Laura was frowning at him, either. Paul cleared his throat. "The mystery wrasse looks like a winner."

"They're really rare," Gregg said in an excited voice.

Laura put her hands on Gregg's shoulders. "Yes. But that's a saltwater fish. We've decided on fresh-water fish."

Paul glanced at the drab fish, then at Laura. "The saltwater fish are so much brighter, more colorful. Look at that blue-and-yellow one."

She was upset. He could see it as she pushed her hair away from her face, a habit of hers when she was tense. It suddenly hit him why. The saltwater varieties were considerably more expensive. And she had spent her money on moving here. That, or she resented spending the money on Gregg.

"I'd like to buy the fish as a welcome present." He remembered the other child. "And something Kirsten wants, too."

"We can't allow you to—"

"Mom, please," Gregg pleaded.

Paul could see that she was torn. Her lovely green eyes darkened as she watched her son. Her feelings played out on her face, he realized. She didn't hide them very well.

"I guess that would be all right," she said finally. "That way we won't have to buy any supplies, since Gregg already has everything for saltwater fish."

She wasn't happy about the decision. That was also transparent. But his responsibility was to the children.

Gregg was careful in his choices, choosing docile species, and Paul had to encourage him to pick out enough fish to fill the tank. So, the boy wasn't spoiled. He hoped that didn't mean that Laura stinted on providing him what he needed. Some women would rather buy new shoes than give their children any extras.

At Paul's urging they also chose some coral and invertebrates. One, the lavender tube anemone, intrigued him. It was so ethereal it barely looked real. The clerk had also pointed them toward live sand for the tank.

"Too bad I can't take these guys to school on Monday." Gregg watched as the clerk scooped one of the fish into a water-filled bag.

"What's up on Monday?" Paul asked.

"We're 'sposed to take a pet, but I don't have a real one, except my fish."

Paul tapped the glass, watching the fish scurry for cover as the clerk continued his search for their purchases. "You want to borrow mine? I have an English setter and he loves going anywhere with kids."

"You mean it?" Gregg jumped so high he nearly careened over the top of the tank. "That would be way cool!" He bounced back toward Laura. "Did you hear that, Mom?"

How could her suggestion of the butterfly collection compare to a dog? "Yes, I did, sweetie."

She listened as Gregg asked for every detail about Paul's dog. She tried to quash the thought that hit her. But…had she replaced one controlling man with another? Paul hadn't bothered to ask her first, to even consider that he ought to. A fraction of her new sense of freedom eroded. And she hated that it had.

* * *

Since Kirsten wasn't interested in anything from the pet store, they took the fish back to the house.

"It's going to take time to set up the tank and acclimate the fish to the new water," Laura told Paul, her voice weary.

"I'm guessing that's something you have to do?"

She held one of the bags carefully. "If you want the fish to survive."

"I thought people owned fish because they were so low maintenance." Paul stared at the clear bag. "I didn't know they were that complicated."

"Most every living thing is," she replied, a shadow closing over her face.

"Is it really going to take all that long?"

"Afraid so. After the tank's set up, we have to float the fish in their bags until the water reaches the same temperature as the new water they'll be released into. Why?"

He motioned to Kirsten. "I don't want her to think I forgot about buying a welcome gift for her."

"She won't." Laura put her purse on the counter. "But, if you'd like, you could take Kirsten to choose something while I help Gregg set up his aquarium."

Paul hesitated. By the time the tank was in place, many of the stores would be closing for the day.

His niece wasn't as old as Kirsten, but he thought

she might like one of the stores on Main Street, too. A small place run by a silversmith. Girls liked jewelry and everything in the store was unique, designed by the owner. The small handcrafted boxes should appeal to a teenager, he guessed.

Kirsten looked skeptical when he parked in front of the shop. Even more surprised when she was sure it was the destination. But he thought it would be a pleasant surprise.

Once inside, she glanced around without much interest.

"Miss Carson designs everything herself."

"Uh-huh."

Well, this clearly wasn't a smart idea.

"Isn't there a mall around here somewhere?"

"Afraid not."

She stared at him. "Really?"

"Really. But we have stores. What kind do you want to go to?"

She toed her sandals. "One with shoes."

"Fine."

Walking down the street, she looked bored with the shops. His niece would be glued to the windows.

When they reached the shoe store, her face fell. "This is it?"

"Yep. Is there a problem?"

She looked at the display in the window. "Where are the designer brands?"

Laura must be a mega shopper. "Probably in San Antonio and Houston."

"No way!"

"Look, Kirsten I know Rosewood isn't what you're used to, but there's a lot to offer here." He didn't add that there was far more to life than shoes since she was already shell-shocked.

"This is a dumpy town and it's all my mother's fault we're here."

He agreed with the last part of her statement, but knew not to voice it. Even though he thought Laura's move was hasty and ill-advised, the family was in Rosewood now. And it was his responsibility to watch out for the kids, not create contention. "She was trying to do something positive for your family. It was hard work moving here, getting settled."

Her eyes narrowed. "A bunch of church ladies did all the unpacking. Why, did my mother say she did it?"

Not exactly. But she didn't tell the truth, either. "That's not the point. It's difficult pulling up stakes, making a new start."

"For all of us!"

"I know, but a mother takes on her children's pain, as well." He expected Kirsten to argue, but she didn't. "You must have other interests besides shoes."

She shrugged. "Music, I guess."

"How about some CDs then?"

"Okay."

The child was unhappy. But he wasn't sure if it was the move or the parenting. He couldn't change Laura, but he could step in to try to fill Jerry's shoes.

On Monday morning, Gregg's classroom was crowded with pets—and parents waiting to take the critters home. The variety was boggling. Dogs, cats, birds, turtles, rabbits, lizards, little furry creatures Laura decided were probably hamsters. She didn't want to think they were any other sort of rodent. Although she had to admit she hadn't seen a hedgehog up close before today.

Despite the lure of a nearby cat who kept eyeing him, Paul's dog, Roddy, remained obediently by his side as his master had ordered. His thumping tail was the only indication of the dog's interest in the other animals.

When it was Gregg's turn to take his pet to the front of the class, he was near bursting with excitement. Laura couldn't hang on to her resentment of being one-upped by Paul when she saw how happy the gesture made her son.

"This is Roddy. He's an English setter," Gregg told his new class proudly.

"Is he really from England?" a dubious girl wearing glasses and keeping a hand on her own dog's head asked. Her poodle wore the same disdainful expression.

Gregg looked at Paul.

Paul stroked Roddy's head. "He was born in San Antonio. But his father's from England."

If possible, Gregg stretched his height up another notch.

"But can he do anything?" The boy who asked had brought his parrot and the bird had shown a remarkable vocabulary.

"Sure!" Gregg said. He and Paul had practiced Roddy's repertoire.

Gregg spoke to the dog in an authoritative tone as Paul had coached him. "Sit."

Roddy sat.

"Up," Gregg commanded.

Up on his hind legs, the large dog was impressive. Most of the kids oohed at the sight.

"Lie down."

Roddy complied.

Gregg formed a mock gun with his fingers. "Play dead."

The dog rolled on his back, looking pretty well dead.

Gregg frowned at the dog as Paul had shown him. "I said *play* dead."

Roddy lifted his head and opened his eyes while maintaining his position.

The kids all laughed.

Gregg snapped his fingers.

Roddy sat up, then bowed his head, eliciting more applause.

The teacher, also clapping, joined them. "That was excellent! What a personality Roddy has. Right, children?"

The kids clapped louder and Gregg beamed.

Paul put his arm on Gregg's shoulders. And something caught in Laura's throat. She didn't have any memories of Jerry sharing a moment like this with his son. He had always been too busy, said it was her job to do the school things with the kids. And look at what he had missed.

Scouting properties was one of Paul's favorite jobs. But that had been before Laura decided to tag along. He thought she'd have given up on the business by now. But leeches had nothing on her.

"We won't be back before school's out," he warned her, stopping the car at the highway cutoff.

She searched in her purse. "Annie said she'd pick up the kids if I was going to be late."

He glanced at her out of the corner of his eye. "Planning ahead?"

"I try to." She located her cell phone, then quickly called Annie who agreed she would keep the children until Laura returned. "I'm set."

Paul couldn't withhold a sigh. And he tried. "Fine." But he didn't plan to entertain her. If she got bored, as he hoped she would, she could just tough it out until they returned that evening.

He headed toward Fredericksburg, a popular Hill Country tourist town. It appealed to well-heeled retirees, and the market was hot. Paul kept his eye on any foreclosures and distress sales that popped up in the vicinity. With increasingly high land values, there was a large profit ratio in securing an older and outdated property, then renovating it for resale. Fortunately Jerry's assistant had stepped up and taken over Jerry's similar work in Houston. It looked as if the man could handle the job permanently.

Laura was quiet as they traveled through the blossoming countryside. The fields were covered with poppies, evening primroses, rocket larkspurs and Engelmann's daisies. Usually this was the time Paul took to collect his thoughts, to forecast his upcoming investments. But, he found his gaze straying over to his companion. He had expected her to rattle on, and her silence was unsettling.

She wasn't one to share her thoughts. And she never spoke of Jerry. Was she that glad he was gone?

They reached Fredericksburg by midmorning. The streets were filled with visitors who had come to the area for the wildflowers and the charm of the German settlement. State-of-the-art medical facilities in the area were another draw for wealthy retirees.

Paul checked his shortlist. A property on ten acres had jumped out at him when he'd prepared the day's agenda. There was also a house near the city center. Paul wanted to see it first.

He found the address easily. Parking in the street, he viewed the chalet-style house. Although the house had nice lines, there was little curb appeal. But the interior could be promising.

As a foreclosure, the place was locked up, but Paul had been doing this long enough to know there was often a way in. He tried the garage door. It hadn't been secured.

"Is this breaking and entering?" Laura whispered.

She looked so concerned that he chuckled. "No. Just entering. It's not posted with No Entry signs so I feel comfortable going in. Plus, I don't intend to steal anything."

"And if it were posted?"

"Then I'd try to see as much as possible through the windows. I can get a feel that way." The disappointing interior was tiny and in poor shape.

"Isn't a two-bedroom, one bath harder to sell?" Laura asked. It wasn't something they had discussed, but she was right.

"Generally, yes. But it might be just the kind of cottage a weekender would like."

She sniffed. "Do you smell that?"

He glanced down at the stained carpets.

"Probably pets. I'd rip out all of this and put in new flooring anyway."

"No, not pets. It smells like mold."

What did she know about mold?

Laura opened a small closet door, then stepped back. "There's been a roof leak, looks like it's been going for a while."

The closet did smell musty. "I'd have to check the attic to be sure."

"My friend, Donna, had toxic mold in her home. It cost a fortune to remediate, then rebuild. You have to hire special recovery companies and their employees wear protective biohazard clothing and masks."

He nodded. "We ran into that in Houston. It was a nightmare. Our budget and time doubled. But I'm not sure that's what we're looking at here."

The living room was covered in wallpaper and the ceiling was painted a dark color. Without electricity, they couldn't turn any lights on to see if there was water damage.

Laura walked into the first bedroom and opened the closet. "This one's musty, too."

Paul located the ceiling access to the attic, then pulled down the foldaway ladder. He was only in the attic a few minutes when he realized Laura was right. All of the timbers were stained. No doubt the Sheetrock beneath the wallpaper was crumbling away.

He climbed back down. "Good call."

"So there is leakage?"

"Massive. The only way this place would make a profit is to get it for near nothing, then demolish and start over." He wiped his hands together. "And that's not likely."

"But you don't know how much it will cost until the auction?"

He knocked the dust and bits of insulation off his clothes. "Sometimes I can find out what the opening bid will be—depends on the trustee. And I abstract the property to find the outstanding liens. That gives me an idea. And that way I make sure there aren't any liens other than the bank's that have to be satisfied."

She pulled her notebook and pen from her purse and began to scribble. "Such as?"

"The IRS is the main one. Most other liens are wiped out with the foreclosure, but not the IRS." He folded up the stairway.

She underlined IRS.

"Once the property's purchased, there aren't any refunds. People have bought second mortgages at foreclosure, thinking they've got a great deal. But they don't realize they still have to pay off the first mortgage." He had to wiggle the folding stairway to make it fit back in place. "And typically you're buying the proverbial pig in a poke. You can't make appointments to view the interiors, so you have to know how to determine square footage from outside.

But the condition is a risk." He pushed lightly on the wall and the Sheetrock gave way. "It's a buyer-beware business."

She wrinkled her nose at the distinctive odor the Sheetrock emitted. "Will we be going to an auction soon?"

The dreaded "we." "There's one in two weeks on the main property I came here to see."

Her face lit up. "Great!"

"But I don't know yet if it's a house I want to bid on."

"Oh… But we still have to look at it, don't we?"

"The place is outside of town." He fingered his keys. "Shouldn't take too long to get there."

Paul had printed directions off the Internet to each address. Although his Land Rover had a navigation system, he preferred to use a map.

The house was much larger than he'd expected. And pinker. The previous owners had terrible taste in color if the exterior was any indication.

As the driveway curved, the rest of the estate swung into view. Barn, stables, guest quarters and a multicar garage.

"Wow." Laura voiced what he was thinking.

Despite the terrible color choice, the architecture was dazzling. Huge panels of glass let in an incredible view of the surrounding hills. Multiple chimneys promised more than one fireplace.

Once parked, they strolled around the grounds. In addition to the pool behind the house, there was also a pond and a creek that bisected the land.

"If this pond had a small pier, fishermen would go nuts!" She knelt next to the reeds and cattails trying to pull one free.

He studied the landscape. "I suppose."

"Don't you think this place would attract buyers?"

"Probably." He made a few notes in his PDA. "But it'll have a hefty price tag."

Giving up on the cattails, she stood up. "But won't the profit potential be higher?"

"Yes," he acknowledged.

They peeked through the windows.

"That's a gourmet kitchen," Laura exclaimed, getting excited. "And it doesn't look as though it's ever been used."

He peered through the French doors. "I'm not sure."

She pointed. "The labels are still on the appliances. You can see the one on the dishwasher the best."

"No one leaves labels on their appliances," he agreed. But it didn't make sense. The house wasn't brand-new. The legal notice had stated that the mortgage to be auctioned off was several years old. Unless... "Maybe this was being fixed up for sale when the owners lost it."

"Does that happen very often?"

"Depends on the reason. If the owners were inexperienced at flipping, they might have taken on more than they could handle." He noticed that the appliances weren't top of the line, which was a bad sign. "They might have overrun their budget and time. Then their financing could have failed if they couldn't repay the note for the renovations."

She continued to stare inside at the impressive kitchen. "You said it was a risky business."

"If you don't know what you're doing. And since I represent several investors, the risk isn't just mine. Flipping can be unpredictable. It's easy to run into unexpected challenges." He moved on to the bay window outside the dining room and frowned. "The color won't work."

"The chandelier's gorgeous." Laura stretched on her tiptoes to try to see in farther. "And paint is fairly cheap, as far as fix-ups go. And look at the marble entry."

He did. But he wanted to get inside.

"I don't see any No Entry signs posted." Laura was checking the windows.

"I doubt you'll find one that's open. With more expensive houses, the bank's rep is more careful with security."

"The laundry room," she murmured. "If we can find that, the window could be unlocked. It's a room you need to vent fairly often and the window's usually small, overlooked."

He stared at her. "Do you have a criminal past I ought to know about?"

She continued to check the locks as they passed each window. "I imagine I've used a laundry room a lot more than you have."

He doubted it. As the eldest growing up, he'd done more than his fair share of laundry.

It didn't take long to locate. And the window *was* unlocked. It wasn't large, but Laura was a small woman and she wriggled through easily. "I'll let you in through the side door."

When he was inside, they toured the main floor, then headed upstairs. The bathrooms had all been updated like the kitchen. But the rooms were all painted terrible colors. And some of the lighting fixtures were just short of horrendous.

"Maybe the owners were color-blind," Laura mused aloud.

"Or they just had bad taste."

She knelt and touched the tumbled marble floor. "I like most of the tile and hardwoods they chose."

"The wood floors would look better if they were stained darker, but that would be easy to do."

She nodded. "Depending on the paint, I guess so—more contrast."

He made more notes. "But you're right, the natural stones are good. So are the bones. It's a great house."

She stood, turning a slow circle to take in the

many windows that looked out to the hills. "Then you're planning to bid on it?"

"I'd extend the deck to take advantage of the million-dollar view, lose some of the cabinets in the kitchen to give access to the porches, add a spa shower in the master bath." He walked closer to one of the windows. "It takes a special clientele to buy something this costly—especially outside of the city—since it would most likely be a second home."

She leaned toward another window, checking how far she could see. "Special clientele, hmm. Like people who want to get out of the city when they can."

"You have someone in mind?"

"Actually, I do."

He was skeptical. "Who?"

"My friend Donna is on the board of the Houston Symphony. We could offer to host a gala at the house and donate the proceeds to the symphony. In exchange, they can play at the gala and give us a copy of their mailing list. Plus, I worked for the auxiliary at the Methodist Hospital. There are quite a few doctors we could invite to an open house. I have contacts with some other organizations I worked with, as well."

He made another note. "I didn't know you did so much volunteer work."

She hesitated. "I needed to fill a lot of hours."

"Surely Jerry and the children took a lot of your time." He looked up from his PDA.

"The children, yes." Then she bit her lip as though she had said too much. "So, what do you think of the 'pink palace'?"

"I like it. The only glitch would be if it doesn't sell fast enough. That could kill the profit, even go the other way."

While she digested what he'd said, he was still thinking about her revelation. And her need to cover it up.

Chapter Six

Paul had already decided to pass on the small cottage. The other home in the area hadn't panned out, either.

But the "pink palace." It could score big or be an equally big bust. They had driven to the county courthouse so he could abstract the title. His hunch had been right. The owners had taken out a large second mortgage to finance the renovations. But since it was from a different lender, that debt would be wiped out in the foreclosure of the first mortgage, which wasn't an unreasonable amount. Of course, he could be contending against a lot of other bidders. That would drive the price up, maybe too far up. But the only way to know was to attend the auction.

It was also held at the county courthouse, on the front steps near the entrance. The antiquated building was fashioned out of native limestone quarried nearby. A tall circular fountain, flanked by dense borders of petunias, bleeding hearts and iris, stood amidst curving stone benches.

He and Laura arrived early but she was too excited by the prospect of her first auction to sit. She had actually squealed when he told her he'd decided to bid on the property. He hadn't told her he wasn't counting on her contacts to sell it. If she really came through, they would be a bonus. But his own Rolodex was filled with enough heavy hitters that there shouldn't be a problem finding a buyer. If he could get the place at the right price. In the week since they had first seen the house, he had checked the tax base so he had a fair idea of the market value and had also consulted with an appraiser.

Laura leaned against one of the benches. "I'm glad you're going to bid on the property."

"I'm not sure about that yet."

That appeared to deflate her. "But, I thought—"

He consulted his notes. "Depends on the opening bid."

"But it's such a great place!"

"Only if I can turn a profit on it."

"Think of the advantages—custom built *and* updated. And the great room's large enough to entertain a big crowd. Not to mention the huge formal areas."

He rocked back on his heels. "And possibly a

huge price tag, which limits the number of potential buyers."

"I have a feeling about this house," she insisted.

"This isn't the only one that'll ever go under the hammer," he reminded her. Texas had one of the highest foreclosure rates in the country.

"No, but I doubt ones like this come along very often."

"True," he admitted, surprised by her fervor. When he'd started the firm he'd gotten equally excited by a promising property.

"Do the auctions start on time?"

"Usually right on the dot. But it depends on the trustee—can't begin without him or her."

She checked her watch. "Only five minutes until takeoff then. And there aren't any other bidders here."

"Yet," he warned. "People show up at the last second."

She began to pace.

But initially only the trustee appeared. However, as he was reading the legal description, another bidder showed, then a second. Two more, in the end. But since more than one property was being auctioned off, it was possible neither was interested in the same one they were.

Laura's anxiety increased visibly. She clutched his arm, her fingers shaking. She acted as though she was truly invested in the proceeding.

Talk died down as the trustee cleared his throat, ready to begin. He announced the lien holder's bid for the property, the amount due the bank.

They were standing only a few feet from the trustee, so Paul didn't even raise his voice as he bid one dollar more.

The balding, portly man standing next to him shifted his overflowing briefcase and entered a bid for a thousand dollars higher.

Laura's fingers dug into his arm.

Paul raised the bid another thousand.

So did the other bidder.

They went back and forth until they had raised the price by twenty-five thousand. But Paul had a figure set in his mind and until he reached it, he intended to keep bidding. So he raised the amount.

And to his surprise, the other bidder shrugged.

He heard the trustee repeat his bid, then, "Going, going, gone."

And the property was his.

Laura's feet left the pavement. "You got it!"

As Paul tendered a certified check for five thousand dollars he couldn't suppress a small grin at her excitement. The entire amount was due in twenty-four hours, but he had investors in place.

"You'll see, this is going to be a super investment." Laura hadn't stopped grinning.

He'd never seen this side of her before. Her first genuine smile.

"I'll contact Donna about the gala and…" she trailed off. "Um, after you figure out how long it will take to paint and refinish the floors, I mean. And the other upgrades."

"I can put together a schedule by the end of the week. There's not that much to do."

She clapped her hands quietly. "Yay."

He reached for his keys. "Did you have time to eat breakfast?"

"Just juice and coffee."

He clicked the remote and the car chirped as the locks popped open. "There's a little German place here that makes great blintzes and kolaches."

Laura reached for the car door. "I was so nervous this morning I barely got some juice down."

She was that concerned about the auction? She wasn't really treating this like a hobby. Of course she had zoned right in on the possible profit from flipping this particular house. Chasing the dollar signs. No wonder she usually looked so unhappy. No one could be content if that was the center of their lives. The Lord was his center and he gave thanks every day for Him.

The restaurant was quiet, the breakfast rush over. Settled in a booth near the window, they watched the bustle in the street. The town was even busy midweek.

"I'm glad Rosewood isn't a tourist spot," she observed, after thanking the waitress for her coffee.

"Yeah. I kept thinking it would get overrun when Fredericksburg became such a hot spot." He put the napkin in his lap. "But now that the premier hospitals have been built here, I think we dodged that bullet."

"You never thought about developing some of the land outside of town?"

"No. I can always make more money. I can't recreate my hometown if it's ruined." He reached for a packet of sugar. "Were you raised in Houston?"

A shadow obscured her eyes. "Yes. I've always lived in the city."

What had spoiled her mood? "I used to wonder what it would be like to grow up in a huge city."

She fiddled with the miniature cartons of cream. "Be grateful you had Rosewood."

"Don't you miss your family?"

She jerked her head up, then searched his face. "We're not close."

He couldn't imagine not being close with family. "So, your parents, they're still alive?"

She stirred her coffee even though it didn't need it. "My mother is."

"But you don't see her much?" He took a swallow of his coffee.

"She and her new husband live in Florida." Two customers passed their table, heading toward the door.

The bell tinkled as the door opened. "How long has it been since your father passed away?"

"He died when I was twenty—eleven years ago." She swallowed. "This isn't the first time she's married since then."

That didn't sound good. "Siblings?"

She emptied more cream into her coffee. "Just me. That's why I wanted to make sure I had more than one child."

"It's lucky you and Jerry were in agreement about that."

She looked out the window at the passing traffic. "Yes."

What was it about her and Jerry? He didn't know, but the joy from the morning had left her expression. She was guarded again. What was she hiding?

Laura tried to rush the kids—both had dawdled getting ready.

"But it's Sunday," Kirsten complained. "We always sleep late on Sunday."

"Not if we want to go to church." Laura tucked her blouse into her skirt.

Kirsten put one bare foot on top of the other. "I *don't* want to go."

"We already had this discussion. Annie and Ethan invited us. I said yes. And we're going."

"Why?"

For a thousand reasons she couldn't voice. A longing to fit in, to experience what she had as a child, to see if she could recapture her belief. And she had been negligent in her children's spiritual education. When Jerry had been alive she hadn't really had a choice. Unless she wanted to be badgered and belittled beyond endurance. But now...

Now it was her responsibility, her choice. And when Annie had urged her to attend, she had felt the first hope in an incredibly long time. Was it possible to find the faith that had sustained her grandmother? Gram was the only positive role model she'd ever had.

And despite her disappointments in her weak son, she'd been a happy woman. She had infused as much joy as she could into Laura's life, as well. She'd made certain Laura had spent as much time as she could out of her parents' home.

With her grandmother, just a ride in the car was an adventure. Because she made it that way. She would stop on a whim at flea markets, and they would try on outrageous hats or search through the stalls for treasures. She'd died when Laura was ten, taking her refuge, her sense of safety, her only link to faith. If her grandmother had lived, Laura had often speculated, perhaps she wouldn't have felt the urgent need to marry Jerry and escape her home. And now that those shackles were gone, she hoped she could reestablish that link.

"Mom. Mom!"

"What is it?"

"Gregg can't find his belt."

Laura rooted through his closet until she found it. The children ready, Laura was both excited and apprehensive as she got them in the car.

Rosewood Community Church was an imposing structure. The steeple towered high into the sky. And the aged brick seemed both graceful and solid. Stained glass windows created a play of light throughout the spacious sanctuary. A large community center was located in the adjacent building.

As they sat, Laura was struck by the beauty of the organ music. Distant memories of sharing a hymnal with her grandmother prompted her to reach for one. She had learned to sing in church, something she had pursued by joining the choir in high school. That had been a long time ago. She had been one of a dozen students who had auditioned for and then made the a cappella performance group, the highlight of her teen years.

"Welcome!" Katherine took the pulpit after the music finished. "Joyful are the songs of the Lord. And joyful are his people." Inclining her head, she led the opening prayer.

Laura listened to the pastor with a hunger she hadn't known she felt. The message on the Lord's guiding hand struck her as something she needed to hear.

Afterward, Katherine welcomed her to the church. "I'm so happy you and your family could be with us today."

"We enjoyed your sermon…especially me."

Katherine clasped her hands. "I hope you'll join us again."

Laura felt a surge of newfound certainty. "We will."

She had only walked a few feet away when Annie and Ethan caught up to her.

Annie shifted her purse and Bible to give Laura a hug. "You came."

Ethan shook hands with Kirsten and then Gregg who grinned, clearly enjoying being treated like an adult.

Within moments, they were surrounded by the women who had helped her unpack and settle in. Along with their husbands and children, they engulfed the Manning family. Then Mandy, the one friend Kirsten had made at school, rushed up. Kirsten's demeanor changed, and she grinned.

"Next time, try to come to Sunday school, too," Annie urged.

"Actually I'd planned on it today, but it took us longer to get ready than I expected." Like wrestling greased pigs.

Ethan winked at Gregg. "The youth activities are fun."

Laura watched Kirsten, who was talking animatedly with Mandy. "You're right."

"There's an activity next week for the teens, a pizza party." Annie consulted her bulletin. "Maybe Kirsten would like to go. I can find out the details if you think she'd be interested."

Laura tried not to squint in the noon sun. "Thanks, Annie."

"I know how important it is for kids to find friends."

"We were sitting behind you during the service." Grace shifted closer. "And you have a lovely voice, Laura. Will you join the choir?"

"It's been years since…" Her murmur trailed to nothing.

"The Lord welcomes us back with loving arms," Grace said gently. "I'm living proof."

Laura choked on something deep inside, then cleared her throat.

Grace lightly clasped Laura's arm. "Think about the choir. You'll find we're a very welcoming congregation."

"Thank you…for everything."

Grace smiled. "I'm happy you've come to Rosewood, Laura. And I think you will be, too. Are we still on for lunch Tuesday?"

"Absolutely." Glancing up, Laura caught sight of Paul. She hadn't seen him inside. He was with a large group of people, laughing and talking. So he had a lot of friends. Just because he was reserved with her didn't mean he was with everyone. He probably didn't have reason to doubt these people. They didn't come with "Jerry" baggage.

She turned back to Annie but not before she'd been spotted. He was at her side a few minutes later.

"We'll see you," Annie said, nodding to Paul as she and Ethan walked away hand in hand. The other women had already scattered to collect their children.

Paul studied her suit. She wished she'd worn something without a designer label. "I didn't expect to see you here."

And why not? Instead she smiled politely. "It's my first visit."

"I hope it'll be one of many."

"Well…I think it might."

He twirled the church bulletin in his hands. "Do you have plans for lunch?"

"Not really, but—" She took a step backward.

He took one forward. "My family always gets together after church, sort of a big potluck. Why don't you bring the kids?"

"I don't know…" She took another step back, realizing too late she'd run out of sidewalk, and one heel sank into the grass.

"My parents want to meet all of you."

"They do?" She put her hand on Gregg's shoulder.

"Jerry was my friend."

"Oh." Of course. Because of Jerry. He had been the one who had received social invitations. Charismatic to everyone but his wife, he'd always won people over. What would his friends have thought if they'd seen the way he bullied and demeaned her? But, of course, he never did when anyone else was around. "Why don't we meet your parents now?" She shaded her eyes as she looked for her daughter. "Kirsten's just over there with her new friend."

Paul gestured toward the parking lot. "They've already left for home. Mom wanted to get a head-start on things."

"She's not expecting us," Laura said, trying to wriggle out of the invitation.

"Doesn't matter." He rolled the bulletin up, then tapped it against his leg. "With five kids, some with their own families, my parents always plan for extra."

Laura was running out of wriggle room.

"Can we go, Mom?" Gregg piped up.

She nearly groaned. At the same time her mind was racing to find an excuse to refuse. Then she glanced over to where Kirsten had been left standing when Mandy went with her parents. Her daughter looked woebegone, and it was her undoing. For all that her in-laws had made Laura's life difficult, Kirsten was missing them. Maybe a day with another family would help. "I suppose we could come. But I don't have anything to bring."

"That's okay. We always have too much."

"We have cheesecake," Gregg announced. "Mom made two."

Laura blinked. "That's right. I made the extra one for Annie and Ethan but I can bring it for lunch and make another one for them later."

He gave her the address and brief directions to the house.

They stopped at home, picked up the cheesecake and then drove to the Russell's house. It wasn't what Laura had expected. She thought they would have an imposing place. True, the house was large, but the well-worn edges seemed to say come in, stay awhile. But they weren't inside yet, Laura reminded herself.

The gardens were filled with rosebushes that appeared to be as old as the house itself.

"This house is old, too," Kirsten complained as Laura rang the bell.

"Don't mention that to our hosts."

Kirsten looked insulted. "I'm not likely to, am I?"

Laura truly didn't know these days. Although she loved her daughter more than life, she was a trial. An unpredictable one.

A mature woman opened the door and Laura realized at once this must be Paul's mother. He favored her, especially his dark eyes. Her smile was wide.

"You must be the Mannings. Welcome. I'm Elizabeth Russell." She ushered them inside.

The home was as welcoming inside as it was outside.

"We sort of clump up in the kitchen and family room," Elizabeth was saying. "But the kids prefer the yard." She turned to the children. "Kirsten, Gregg, what would you prefer?"

Kirsten shrugged, but Gregg was decisive. "Outside."

"Why don't I introduce you to the other kids?" Elizabeth looked at Laura. "Our oldest grandchild is six, so Kirsten might prefer to stay with us."

"That sounds like fun," Laura said.

Kirsten brightened.

Her child was growing up. Despite her tantrums and willfulness. Laura stroked Kirsten's soft hair.

Kirsten looked up startled, but Laura didn't remove her hand.

Elizabeth pointed the way to the kitchen and then left to introduce Gregg to his new playmates. Laura carried in the cheesecake.

The room was buzzing with activity, overflowing with casserole dishes, bowls and platters. Sunlight flooded the classic black-and-white tile, pooled on the well-worn, round oak table that sat in the center of the room.

"Hi, you must be Laura and Kirsten." A pretty

woman, who was visibly pregnant, took the Tupperware container. "Thanks. I'm Jennifer, Paul's sister. My children and husband are out back." She pointed to another woman across the room who shared her pretty looks. "This is my sister, Sharon. The blond dynamo is my sister-in-law, Robin." She pointed to an older woman at the far counter. "My aunt Eloise. And, if that's not enough people to remember, our grandparents are outside, too."

"It's great to meet you all. What can we do to help?"

"What do you have there?" Jennifer asked, eyeing the covered dish.

"Cheesecake."

"Be still my heart." Jennifer put her hand to her chest. "Let's get that to a safe place. We could use help in the dining room. I think everyone's here now so we can put the leaves in the main table and set up the kids' table." She added to Kirsten, "You're at the adult table I think."

Kirsten straightened up, pleased to be included with the adults.

It was a large group, but the dining room was spacious. One of the advantages of the old Victorian homes, they were built when family and friends sat down to big dinners.

Elizabeth returned just as the tables were in place. "Thanks for doing this. I'll get out the linens." She retrieved a starched white tablecloth and napkins from the sideboard. "I know it's not trendy, but I love setting the table with my best linens and dishes. The girls tell me it wouldn't be a crime to use paper plates, but I just can't bear to."

"I like tradition. My grandmother always did the same thing on Sundays." Most of the time it had just been the two of them since Laura's bickering parents hadn't wanted to attend.

She helped Elizabeth smooth out the tablecloth, then reached for the stack of plates already set out on the sideboard. She traced a finger around the edge of the familiar blue willow pattern.

"I'm sorry about the last-minute invitation," Elizabeth said as she handed some glasses to Kirsten. "Would you like to fill these with ice?" As Kirsten complied, Elizabeth turned back to Laura. "Paul told us all about you, and we've been anxious to meet your family."

Considering Paul knew almost nothing about them, Laura couldn't help wondering what he could have had to say. "It's gracious of you to have us."

Elizabeth laughed. "I hope you still think so after the entire mob is here."

To Laura's way of thinking, they already had a mob. "Do you expect many more?"

"My youngest son, Kevin, is in town, but he's stopping by a friend's before lunch."

"So he doesn't live in Rosewood?"

"He's in medical school—Baylor in Houston," Elizabeth said with pride. "He and our youngest daughter, Sharon, are both still in school. She's studying law."

An entire family of overachievers. "I met Sharon in the kitchen."

Elizabeth hesitated. "I know it can be daunting getting acquainted in a new town. If we can make that any easier, I hope you'll turn to us. When Paul was a boy, my husband was serving in Vietnam. It's not the same as being widowed, but I know how difficult it is to parent alone."

Laura struggled to find an appropriate reply. She and Jerry had never parented together. "Kirsten, in particular, really misses her father."

"I'm sure you all do."

"Yes." It was harder and harder to keep up this pretense of missing the man who had made her so unhappy. But these were Jerry's friends.

"Paul should be here any minute. He always brings a cooler with soft drinks for the kids. He likes to spoil them."

A side of her partner she hadn't expected. "It's hard not to spoil children. If I could, I'd give mine everything, but…"

"It's a balancing act, that's for sure. But your kids seem well-grounded."

Laura glanced toward the kitchen where Kirsten

was. "For the most part." It was tempting to pour out the truth to this sympathetic woman. But Laura wasn't used to easy confidences.

"Paul tells me you're learning how to flip houses."

Laura searched the other woman's expression but didn't see any hidden meaning. "After I've interned I'll be able to support my children."

Elizabeth leaned toward her. "I don't mean to pry, but I was under the impression that Jerry left a secure estate for the children."

Laura could've kicked herself. She was leaking too much personal information. "I want to be independent." She couldn't keep a trace of fierceness from her tone.

"I've worked for years, you know." Elizabeth folded a napkin. "I'm a librarian. Doesn't sound very exciting, but I love it. The jobs's been flexible and helped a lot, especially during the lean times when Charles was recuperating."

Laura cleared her throat. "Recuperating?"

"He had one operation after another on his back and legs when he got back from the war. And until Paul started helping us out I'm not sure what we'd have done without my income."

"Paul helped you?"

"He still does." Elizabeth folded another napkin. "He's put all his brothers and sisters through college. Now Sharon and Kevin with law and medical school. Neither is married and Paul wants to make sure they both get their full education."

Sobered, Laura realized she knew very little about her mentor. "That's admirable."

Elizabeth studied two serving bowls, choosing the larger one and putting the other back in the sideboard. "For him, it's just family."

Laura couldn't imagine such a thing. Her own parents didn't know anything about family. And Jerry's parents had always had an agenda. "I see."

Elizabeth put a spoon into the yellow serving bowl. "I'm lucky. My parents and Charles's are still with us. Their health is on the decline, but…" Her eyes watered. "I'm sorry. I get pretty emotional when I think about how fortunate we are."

Laura placed a gentle hand on the other woman's arm. "Don't apologize. I'd give anything to still have my grandmother."

"You lost her when you were young?"

Remembering more acutely than she wanted, Laura nodded.

"I'm sorry. That must have been hard."

Her sympathetic, understanding tone was nearly Laura's undoing. Biting her lip, she nodded again.

Elizabeth draped an arm around Laura's shoulders. "I'm sure she's watching over you now."

Laura wished she could be that sure. She still

questioned why the Lord had allowed her to meet Jerry, to couple her life with his.

"I see Mom's put you to work."

Paul's voice as he stood beside the dining room table was so unexpected Laura jumped.

"But she's usually not a demanding overseer," he added, not hiding his curiosity.

"You startled me," Laura explained.

Paul looked first at Laura, then his mother.

"I was just telling Laura that you tend to spoil your nieces and nephews," Elizabeth said, trying to smooth the awkward moment.

"Kids are meant to be treated special."

Elizabeth glared at her son. "I don't think they're missing out on anything."

Laura watched the two, in ways so very alike. And wondered at the undercurrent. They were both quiet, having reached some kind of silent truce. "I know my two will enjoy them," Laura said.

Paul stared at her blankly.

"The sodas. I don't let them have as many as they'd like. It may be old-fashioned but I don't think all that sugar's good for their teeth." Laura tensed, not certain how to end her rambling. "My grandmother always felt that way and it's stuck with me all these years. So, anyway, the soda will be a treat for them."

"Well…I hope they like the ones I picked." He

rubbed his hands together. "I see you have the tables all set up. Any word on Kevin, Mom?"

Elizabeth shook her head. "He'll probably be here soon, and I won't be surprised if he brings a friend or two." She turned to Laura. "My children have always brought their friends home to meals, so I've learned to prepare plenty."

Laura positioned **a plate on** the table. "We've stretched that quite a bit."

"Not in the least. I was hoping Paul would ask you. Has he told you about story hour at the library? Gregg would enjoy it."

Elizabeth gave her the details. As she did, Laura watched Paul leave the dining room. But not before he sent her a questioning look. Now what?

Charles sat at the head of the table. Bowing his head, he clasped the hands of those seated next to him and blessed the meal and all who were present. A hearty amen rippled around the room.

Steaming dishes began their journey, passed from hand to hand as everyone dug in to the big spread. Other than at charity functions, Laura had never lunched with so many people. But the Russells seemed to take it all in stride. Laughter and conversation crisscrossed the room like well-placed sabers in a military procession. There seemed no end to the topics or the opinions trotted out for discussion.

And although both sets of grandparents were frail, they were treated the same as everyone else. Kirsten and Gregg drank in the unfamiliar experience with wide eyes.

And Charles had insisted that Laura sit beside him. Jennifer sat on her right side. Laura learned she was the second oldest child after Paul. "There are five years between Ben, who's a year younger than me, and Sharon. Then another two years to Kevin. He's the baby at twenty-two. We're really proud of him. He's going to Baylor Med."

"And Ben is...?"

Jennifer pointed across the table to a lean, handsome man who resembled Paul. "His wife's next to him, Robin. They have two boys. He and I are the only ones with children so far. I guess you know about Paul, why he's not—" she lowered her voice even though the surrounding conversation guaranteed her words couldn't carry down to him "—you know..."

Laura didn't, but she wasn't bold enough to ask.

"Sharon wants to finish law school before she gets married, and Kevin's not even thinking about a family yet. He knows how hard it would be to combine one with med school, then interning and residency."

Laura kept her voice low, too. "And Paul pays for their schooling?"

Jennifer scooped some macaroni salad on her plate. "He put all of us through school." She patted the small mound of her tummy. "I'm a stay-at-home mom now, but my husband is a teacher. You met Alec, didn't you?"

Laura glanced down the table at the redheaded man who was teasing Paul's grandmother, making her laugh. "Before dinner."

"I have my teaching degree, and I plan to use it when the kids are in school." She patted her stomach again. "Of course, that'll be a while. This little one's not due for quite a while. Until I met Alec, I'd planned to help Paul put the younger kids through school."

Buttering a roll, Laura thought about Paul's plans, whether he had put them aside for his siblings.

Charles passed a dish of olives. "Is Jennifer talking your ear off?"

Laura took the hand-painted porcelain tray. "Not at all."

He laughed. "Our dinners are rarely dull. When the kids were growing up it seemed like there was a new crisis every day. And Jennifer brought home every stray animal in the county. When she left for college I thought that would stop. But Kevin had the same inclination."

"Could that be why he's chosen medicine?"

"I used to think he'd be a vet. But he'd rather use people for his guinea pigs." His eyes sparkled.

"You must be proud of your children."

His fingers curled around a water glass. "Paul's

made my dreams for them possible. Have you gotten to know him yet?"

Had she? "I don't suppose so. Not really. During the day I'm trying to absorb everything. The responsibility of spending other people's money is rather..."

"Daunting?"

"Exactly. Paul's so experienced he knows what's going to be profitable by second nature." She plucked at the linen napkin covering her lap. "When I said I wanted to learn, I don't think I really grasped how elusive the bottom line could be."

"I think that's what made it exciting for Paul." Charles sat back in his chair. "At least at first. But, I'm sure as you learn, you'll get more confident."

She wasn't sure. "I hope so. He makes it look effortless." She pushed at the hair on her forehead. "He did warn me it would be difficult..."

"Any new job is. When I was in pilot training I'd dream every night about what we'd learned that day." His smile was bittersweet. "Didn't think I'd ever remember what I needed to. But once it sank in, it was like another skin. Couldn't shed it for love or money."

Hesitating, Laura bit her lip. "Do you miss it? Flying, I mean?"

"In a lot of ways."

Laura was afraid she'd said too much, prodded in a private area. "I'm sorry. I didn't mean to bring up uncomfortable memories."

Charles shifted in his chair. "They're not all bad memories. I'm proud to have served my country. Would I have chosen to be shot down? No. But I got to come home, and a lot of men didn't. I'm sorry it's been hard on my family, but I've got the best wife and family a man could ask for."

"Elizabeth has been so welcoming." Laura waved toward the others. "So has everyone else. I appreciate today's invitation."

"We were curious about you."

She swallowed. "Me?"

He patted her hand. "Don't look so alarmed. It takes a lot of guts to make a new start, especially after you'd just lost your husband."

Settling the kids, especially Kirsten, in new schools had been trying. Knowing they missed their friends still made her feel guilty. And Kirsten never let her forget how unhappy she was. "I suppose."

"No two ways about it."

"I've never felt very brave," she confessed.

He leaned forward. "The courageous seldom do. Only fools never feel fear. And you don't strike me as a fool."

Laura's eyes stung. Her father had never encouraged her, never made her feel competent. "Thank you."

He patted her hand again. "Can I give you some advice?"

She nodded.

"Try not to be so wary. Things will work themselves out. New town, new home, new job—that's a lot to tackle at once. Your children seem to be doing fine."

Laura wished that were true. "Gregg's adjusting, but Kirsten…"

"Teenage years are the hardest. All of my children were trials. We were uprooted in a way, too. My surgeries were in San Antonio and that was a lot of going back and forth. School events, parties, football games—those dates don't change because your parents have something else on the burner. But they adjusted. Has Kirsten made many new friends?" He stretched his legs and Laura wondered if his pain was constant.

"Just one so far. She had so many back in Houston—kids she'd known since elementary school. I remember being her age. It wasn't easy."

Charles lifted his coffee cup. "My voice was changing about then. I was in constant fear that I'd croak at the worst possible moment. And girls terrified me."

Still a handsome man, she would have thought he'd always been confident, sure of himself.

Jennifer, overhearing his last remark, laughed. "Hard to believe, Dad."

"You and your sister scared me the worst. Not every guy out there is like your Alec."

"Oh, Daddy." Jennifer patted Laura's arm. "You must think we're all soppy. It's mainly my hormones."

"Don't believe it, Laura. She's always been soppy." His eyes twinkled.

Jennifer passed the rolls across the table. "Ask him who helped when I brought home all those stray animals."

"She always hid them in the garage," Charles replied. "And who was most likely to be in the garage, I ask you?"

Jennifer laughed. "Why do you suppose I *put* them in the garage?"

Laura laughed, as well. As she did, she caught Paul's inquisitive look from the other end of the table. Elizabeth had seated Kirsten between herself and Paul. Together they made sure the child was part of the conversations that kept hopping around the room.

Sharon waved her mother down as she picked up the basket and started to retrieve more rolls. "I'll get them, Mom."

As she did, Robin checked again on the children's table. Laura could spot a few messes there, but no one seemed to mind. The kids giggled a lot, but nothing riotous. It was amazing she felt so comfortable in a home she'd just set foot in for the first time that day.

She felt a hand on her shoulder. "Would you like some more iced tea?" Sharon asked. "Or coffee?"

"Tea, but I can get it."

"Gives me a chance to stretch my legs. I spend the whole week running between classes, papers and exams, and I always feel like I've entered another time zone when I come home." She took Laura's glass. "Jen, how 'bout you?"

"I'm reached my caffeine limit for today." She didn't look too happy about the fact.

"I'll root around the kitchen. Do you want some juice?"

As she decided, Charles caught Laura's attention. "Paul tells me he didn't know you very well, either, before your move."

Or now. "We didn't see much of one another. He came to an occasional party at our house, but living in different cities, he and Jerry did most of their communication by phone."

"Paul never has cared for big cities. And Houston's traffic…well, I don't have to tell you. He said it reminded him of a giant anthill that someone had stirred with a stick. Too many people." Charles lifted his coffee cup. "I don't think I could live there, either. Did you like it?"

"I didn't really know anything else until I moved here," she said. "It was my home and the city has a lot to offer, but…" She couldn't very well blurt out that she felt more at home in Rosewood than in all her years in Houston.

"More ham, Laura?" Jennifer offered the large platter.

"I'm almost stuffed." She laid a hand over her stomach. "Everything's delicious, but I don't think I can eat much more."

"You have to!" Jennifer exclaimed. "Well, you don't *have* to, but we're going to have dessert outside in a little while. I've seen the preview and it all looks yummy. I have my name on a piece of your cheesecake."

"I hope it'll be okay," Laura worried. Jerry had never cared for her cooking. Like everything else she did. She sometimes wondered if he was being too critical, but he had come from a family with breeding and background. Which she had not, as he had reminded her often enough.

Jennifer replaced the platter of ham in the center of the table. "Your cheesecake looks fantastic. And I can hardly wait to get into it. Pregnancy does that to me. At least that's my excuse."

Sharon put their drinks on the table. "She always has an excuse. Jen has a sweet tooth a mile long."

"Thanks."

Sharon tapped her sister's head. "We love you anyway."

As the dinner wound to a close, the siblings

gathered dishes and carried them into the kitchen. By virtue of age and respect, the grandparents kept their seats as the younger generation cleared the table.

"I'm glad it's sunny outside," Paul said, jostling past Laura with an armful of plates. "Spring here can be pretty unpredictable."

Ben grinned as he came through to the kitchen holding the platter of ham above his head so Jen's dog couldn't get at it. "Our big brother worries about everything that's not under his control—even the weather."

He really was a control freak? Like Jerry?

Laura watched as Kirsten, relaxed enough to let down her guard, went outside with the younger children. Being a grown-up for too long was a strain.

A sudden flurry of plastic wrap and aluminum foil ensued.

Once the perishables were stowed in the refrigerator Elizabeth herded them all outside. "Let's enjoy the day—the dishes can wait."

Adirondack chairs and gliders were scattered around the large yard. At one end of the lawn, a soccer net had been set up.

"Your family's amazing," Laura told Paul quietly as they stood in the backyard beneath massive oak trees.

He picked up an acorn and tossed it across the yard. "I think so."

"The kids are really enjoying this. Kirsten's been

restless since her father died. Jerry's parents were a connection to him."

"You make it sound as though everything's in the past—even your relationship with the Mannings."

She plucked at the leaves on a low-hanging branch. "Things aren't the same as they used to be. And even if I wanted to change that I couldn't."

His eyes narrowed. "Sometimes you sound as though you're hiding some huge secret."

Laura could no longer swallow. The lump in her throat had grown too large. "Everyone has some sort of secret."

"I don't."

"Really?" She shredded the leaves in her hands. "You never mentioned putting your siblings through school."

A gleam lit his eyes. "So we're confiding in each other now?"

Tactical error. She looked at the ground.

"And I don't consider helping my brothers and sisters a secret." His mouth thinned. "Although my fiancée thought it was a crime."

Startled, Laura released the leaves she'd picked. "A crime?"

"She said we needed to finance our lives, not my siblings. It was a pretty nasty breakup."

"That's terrible. Were you engaged long?"

"Long enough." The breeze carried the scent of

roses and fresh brewing coffee. The kids hollered as one of them made a goal on the far end of the yard. "Two years. I thought she was the one.… So, what's yours? This secret everyone has?"

Pain lodged in her chest and she wished she could pour it all out to him. "It's nothing that grand, nothing even…important."

He studied her. "You're not very convincing."

She'd always been a poor liar. Her grandmother had said she wore the truth like a flag and a lie as though it were a blister. Her face would flame with revealing warmth and she always thought she would burst under close examination.

But now wasn't the time. There was too much at stake. If Paul got mad, he could refuse to teach her. And there wouldn't be much she could do about that if he did. Even new starts weren't completely new, she was realizing. Because the past had come along with her. She couldn't shake it off, or outrun it. Her sigh was as heavy as the darkening clouds.

"That sounded ominous."

"Sorry. I didn't mean it that way."

"Why the sigh?"

"Just thinking about new starts…" She shook her head. "They're not all they're cracked up to be."

"Tiring of Rosewood already?"

"Oh, no!" She reached again for the branch, needing to do something with her nervous hands.

"There's something intangible here…something that…warms me."

"I've heard people say it's like a place from another time. And I think maybe that's okay."

Grateful that he didn't mock her sentiment, she cautiously raised her head. "The community, the people…it reminds me of when I was little…with my grandmother."

"You were close?"

"She was incredible." And no one had ever taken her place in Laura's heart. "But we've all lost somebody important."

"Like Jerry?"

"Yes." The solitary word came out in a mumble.

Paul continued to study her, but for all that was in her, Laura couldn't dredge up any remorse.

His disappointment couldn't have been more obvious. And that bothered her more than it should.

Chapter Seven

Paul lingered after the others had all gone home. He couldn't get Laura's face out of his thoughts. Even though his friendship with Jerry hadn't remained as close as it had been in college, he keenly felt the loss. And yet his widow didn't. How could she run so hot and cold?

His mother tinkered with the last of the meal's remains in the kitchen.

"I thought your volunteers washed the dishes."

Elizabeth continued wiping the tile counter. "They did, but I have my own way of putting everything back. You're here longer than I expected. Not that I'm complaining."

He reached for one of her homemade pecan sandies. "Yeah."

"Something on your mind?"

"Laura Manning."

"I thought so." She poured a glass of milk and handed it to him. "You haven't got her figured out and it's bothering you."

"I get the impression she's glad Jerry's dead."

Elizabeth was quiet for a moment. "Maybe she is." She rinsed out the sponge, then dried her hands on the skirt of her apron. "Maybe she has reason to be."

"Mom!"

"You don't know what goes on between two people behind closed doors, son. I sensed a lot of sadness in that girl…and something's causing it. She looks so beaten down. And for someone that young…" She wiped the counter again, not really seeing it. "It's not natural. She's wounded, I think."

"But—"

"Other than work, you and Jerry didn't see much of each other after school, did you?"

"No. Still…"

She leaned against the stove. "I don't want to conjecture, but I think you ought to keep an open mind about her."

He reached for another cookie. "You didn't think she was pushy?"

His mother crinkled her brow. "Should I have?"

"Well, the way she came to town…then insisted on horning in at the office."

"Were you going to offer her a position?"

Brushing the crumbs from the counter, he slid them onto a paper napkin. "No."

"Then I guess she didn't have much choice, did she?" Elizabeth wiped down the salt and pepper shakers. "She says she wants to provide for her children."

Paul frowned. "Jerry left enough money that she doesn't have to."

"Money you're controlling?" She put the sponge down and poured more milk into his glass.

"Yes."

She pursed her lips. "Hmm."

"Jerry must have had good reason for setting up the trust that way."

She was quiet.

"Mom?"

"I think you need to get to know Laura better."

"Maybe."

Elizabeth cocked her head. "Maybe?"

He sighed. "Okay. Open mind."

"She's not Britney."

His ex-fiancée, who had made money the center of her life. And he had never suspected it when they met. But once they were engaged, she began by having her ring appraised, supposedly for insurance. But when she suggested another diamond cut would be more flattering, he should have known. He had his first hint when she sweetly suggested, while they were at the jewelers, that a larger stone might be a better investment since it was a ring meant for a lifetime. Laura might not be Britney, but he had his suspicions about her.

Elizabeth reached for the plate of cookies. "I'll wrap these up for you to take home."

He filched one more. "This ought to do me."

"I don't think so, son. You're going to have a lot to chew over. Might as well enjoy doing it."

The following morning, Laura was already in, seated at her desk and on the phone when Paul arrived at the office.

He poured himself a cup of coffee as he listened to her side of the conversation. Sounded as if she was making calls concerning the open house they planned for the costly Fredericksburg property. So she wasn't letting that slide. One point for his mother.

He thumped down in his ancient wooden chair. But then, if they made a big profit, a percentage went into her children's half of the company. Point for him.

Laura replaced the phone on the receiver. "Five down, thirty to go."

He dug through the bottom drawer for his listing file. "I'm going back to Fredericksburg. I have a few more properties to look at. Need to check the progress on the pink palace. My local contractor's reliable, but I want to make sure we're on schedule."

Laura immediately started pulling the papers on her desk into a stack. "Should we take the paint chips along?"

He flipped open the file. "The decorator's going to meet me there, she'll have some. I have to choose the exterior color first. I want it painted as soon as possible so the landscaper can get to work."

She swiveled around in her chair to face him, powering down her computer, a laptop she had brought to the office herself. "Will there be much landscaping?"

"What's there now is overgrown and outdated." He stirred the coffee. "No one wants hedgerows anymore. Curb appeal sucks the buyer in."

She was a nodding sponge, soaking up everything he taught her. Abruptly she stopped nodding. "Is it all right for me to tag along?"

"What about the kids?"

"I can make a quick call."

It didn't take long to learn that Annie would have been willing. She had made a blanket offer to watch the kids whenever necessary. But she had plans for the afternoon.

When Laura reported this, crestfallen, he remembered his mother's advice. *Get to know her better.* Well, if that's what she wanted… "Why don't I call my mother, see what she's doing this afternoon?"

"I couldn't impose—"

"I can." He grinned. He was just doing what his mother had asked him to. He shouldn't be the only one to make sacrifices. Elizabeth was agreeable, if a little startled by his request.

Once in Fredericksburg, Paul stopped at the project in progress first. He had barely pulled up in the circular drive when the decorator arrived.

Sleek, sophisticated, she was an uncommonly attractive woman. Paul introduced them. Allison was cool, appraising her. Laura tugged at her casual blouse, wishing she'd chosen something more flattering. The other woman had the ability to make her feel like a mouse in less than a minute.

As they consulted on the color, Paul turned to Laura. "What do you think?"

Glad to have Allison's eyes on something other than her, she pointed to a soft cream nearly the color of newly churned butter. "This one."

The decorator used a wickedly long fingernail to tap another chip. "This brown brings out the umber in the stone. And it'll make the house recede, become part of the landscape."

Laura studied the color, remembering what she had learned. "Which might be fine for an established owner, but when selling, don't you want the house to pop?" She directed the question to Paul.

"Laura's right, Allison. Let's go with her

choice. It'll work well with the lighter color in the stone, as well."

Allison didn't look happy, but she clipped the paint chip to her notebook. "About the appliances—I'd like to replace them all. I worked up the cost."

"But they're brand-new!" Laura protested.

"High-end buyers want high-end appliances," Allison retorted. "And in a house this size we need double Sub-Zero refrigerators and the same with dishwashers."

"Right," Paul agreed. "I'd already figured them into the budget."

Deflated, Laura was silent. This *was* why she had come along—to learn. But faced with the predatory Allison, Laura hated for her ignorance to show. Trailing them, she listened, but she didn't offer any more opinions. However, she didn't really disagree with the rest of the woman's suggestions, either.

When they caught up with the contractor, Laura thought Allison would excuse herself. But the woman stuck by Paul's side. Laura had no idea why this bothered her.

Maybe this was their usual relationship, but it seemed odd to Laura that the decorator felt the need to be in on every detail. Allison hung on even when they met with the landscape designer and it was clear she wasn't needed in the discussion. Laura's feminine intuition told her Allison wasn't interested in real estate details. She was interested in Paul.

Not that the woman seemed like his type. She was too…brittle. And artificial. Laura knew she wasn't an expert on what he preferred but she couldn't imagine Allison mingling with his family or the friends of his she'd met at church.

As much as she liked the "pink palace," Laura was glad when they climbed into Paul's Land Rover and left.

"You're quiet," he commented as they drove toward town.

She shrugged. "Nothing to say I suppose."

"It's been my experience that when a woman claims that, she has plenty to say."

Laura straightened in her seat. "You say that as though you've known hundreds."

He laughed, huge and hearty in the confines of the vehicle. "Should I be flattered?"

"Not especially."

"Okay, I give. Why do you sound so huffy?"

"Huffy?" Laura straightened even further, realizing as she did that her spine must be aligned perfectly by now. Embarrassed, she tried to relax. "I wasn't aware that I sounded huffy."

"Definitely huffy."

"You're imagining things."

He tapped the steering wheel. "I have a good

imagination—just ask my nieces and nephews. I'm great at make-believe. But this is real."

Realizing she had been caught out, Laura sighed. "If I sound huffy, I'm sorry. There's no reason."

He shook his head. "Not buying it."

She wished they would arrive in town so she had something, anything to distract him with. "It's really none of my business."

"What isn't?"

"Allison. Your relationship with her, I mean."

He frowned. "She's my decorator. Nothing there to examine."

Laura cleared her throat.

Paul flicked on his turn signal. "You don't think so?"

"*She* doesn't think so."

Paul chuckled. "Now who has the well-tuned imagination?"

She rolled her eyes.

"You really think that Allison…?"

"Yep."

"I wish you hadn't told me."

"Why?"

He kept his concentration on the road. "Don't you see? Now I'll feel awkward every time I have to work with her. And she's terrific. Talented designers in the middle of the Hill Country aren't a dime a dozen. In fact, they're hard to find. Especially ones who know what makes a house sell."

Laura looked out the window. She'd had to open her mouth. "Um, didn't you say we had more properties to look at?"

He turned down another small road. "They're in town. One sounds especially promising. After we look at them, we can grab some lunch."

Grateful he'd let the other subject go, Laura pulled out her notebook. Still, she couldn't resist sneaking another glance at his handsome profile. Just that jaw alone...No wonder the decorator was interested in him.

"Mom?" Kirsten looked up from tearing the lettuce.

Laura turned off the faucet, wiping her hands. "Yes?"

"There's going to be a pizza party this week."

"Oh?" The one Annie had mentioned.

"Mrs. Russell said it ought to be fun."

Could it be that Kirsten was listening to an adult who was a positive influence? "I agree."

"You do?"

"Sure. It'll be a fun way to meet some other kids."

Kirsten shrugged, but Laura could see she was interested. Instead of pushing, she peeled a cucumber.

"So, I can go if I want?" Kirsten made her voice deliberately casual.

Laura hid her grin. "I think that'd be okay." She reached for a tomato. "I could help you pick out something to wear."

Kirsten rolled her eyes. "I don't think so."

When her daughter had been a toddler, Laura had dressed her in lacy pink dresses. Kirsten had been so much easier then.

"Mom?" Gregg scooted into the room, all energy and squeaking tennis shoes.

"Hi, sweetie. What's up?"

"Can we go to the park?"

"Any special reason?"

"I need to practice ball. And they've got fields and everything there."

"Everything?"

"Batting cages and nets. You know."

She had never been proficient in sports. She had felt lucky to escape from high school P.E. alive. Jerry, being a sports whiz, had berated this short-coming. "I guess we could if we have a quick dinner. The lasagna's done." She looked at her daughter. "What do you say, Kirsten?"

"I don't know…"

Gregg tapped his sister lightly on the shoulder. "Come on."

Kirsten rolled her eyes again. "I guess we have to keep the squirt happy."

After a fast dinner, they headed over to the park.

Gregg was right. The baseball field was large and well planned. But it was the rest of the space that impressed Laura. The duck pond was bordered by alternating rows of flowers and hedges. Tall, leafy trees provided lots of shade. In addition to the playground equipment, picnic tables were scattered throughout the park. And in the center, on a gently sloping hill, stood a large, graceful wooden gazebo. Laura could just imagine the weddings that took place here. And maybe old-fashioned concerts, she mused.

"Mom." Gregg tugged on her sleeve. "Let's go over there." He pointed to the baseball field.

"Okay."

They had barely started practicing when people began to gather. Men wearing matching T-shirts walked onto the field.

"Honey, I think they may be here to play a game," Laura said to Gregg.

His face fell. "You mean we can't practice?"

She looked around the field. "I don't know."

"Look, Mom. There's Paul."

So it was. He should know what was going on. She waved.

"Hey, what you two doing here?" he said, coming over.

"I need to pitch and stuff," Gregg replied.

"Is there going to be a game?" Laura asked.

"It's a practice game, won't last too long. Maybe

you'd like to watch. After it's over, I could toss the ball around with Gregg."

"Cool!" Gregg enthused.

Maybe it should bother her that Gregg was willing to ditch her; instead she was relieved. She wasn't any good at baseball. She only did it because Jerry had never taken the time with Gregg.

"Thank you. Gregg will enjoy playing with someone who knows what they're doing."

Paul pointed to a small wooden structure close to the bleachers. "The Snack Shack should be open. Not a big variety, but you'll find cold drinks, Popsicle ices, hot dogs."

Gregg immediately looked in that direction and Laura chuckled. "Maybe later. We just had dinner."

Paul flexed his glove. "I'd better get into position. See you after the game."

"Good luck," Laura replied. As he loped across the field, she wiggled the bill on Gregg's cap. "Go and get your sister." Kristen had lingered by the duck pond.

"Okay." He took off at a run across the park.

Kirsten, still in a good mood, didn't object to watching the practice. Although the game didn't count toward the season, the men played as though it did. Laura noticed that Paul was a natural, running fast, hitting base runs and even one homer. Gregg was impressed, jumping up and down and hollering out encouragement. By the time the game was over, he was pumped about his new tutor.

Despite having played nine innings, Paul was still energetic as he and Gregg took to the batting cages.

"It's considerate of Paul to take the time for Gregg," Laura mused.

"I guess so." Kirsten replied, beginning to get restless.

"I know this move has been tough for you, sweetie. But I think things will get better as you make more friends."

Kirsten toed her shoes against the bleacher step. "I still wish we didn't have to come here."

"You know how proud you were of your dad?"

Frowning, Kirsten nodded.

"I want you to be that proud of me, too. And that wasn't going to happen if we stayed in Houston." She took a deep breath. "I don't want to burden you with the problems your dad and I had." As a child, hearing her parents fighting constantly, often deep in the night when she should have been sleeping, Laura had promised herself she would never do the same to her children. "But Daddy set up his will so that I have only a small allowance. Not enough for me to have gone to school to get an education."

Kirsten was shocked. "Why'd he do that?"

Laura licked her lips, afraid to say too much, but knowing that sparing her daughter hadn't worked, either. "Your dad had…control issues. And I never wanted to upset the family by fighting with him, so I let most of them slide. And, I'm afraid he still wants to control things…even though he's gone."

Kirsten jumped up. "You make him sound mean!"

Laura stood, as well. "I loved your father." That was true at one time. "But none of us is perfect."

Kirsten's big blue eyes filled with tears. "I miss him."

Laura grasped her shoulders, drawing her close. "Of course you do, sweetie. You're supposed to. Never doubt that he loved you."

Pulling away after a few moments, Kirsten rubbed her eyes, wiping away the tears. Laura smoothed the hair that fell across her forehead.

"So we moved here because of money?"

"That and because I truly wanted us to have a new start. Can you understand that?"

Kirsten's lips trembled, but her expression remained troubled. "I don't know. I don't want to just forget about Daddy."

Laura hated to see her child in pain. "I wouldn't want you to. In fact, I thought it might be fun to make a memory scrapbook. What would you think about that?"

"Okay, I guess."

"We can go through all the old pictures and clippings." Laura made sure she sounded enthusiastic. "And you could make one for Nana and Grandpa, too."

Kirsten's looked up eagerly. "When are we going to see them?"

Laura wasn't ready for that yet. "I'm not sure. We'll have to talk to them."

"They said you didn't have to come here and work in Daddy's business."

Laura smoothed her hair. "We don't always agree, sweetie. But I wouldn't have taken you and Gregg away from your friends if I hadn't thought this was necessary."

"Nana said you were just thinking about yourself."

Stung, Laura was silent for a moment. "And what do you think?"

Kirsten bent her head. "I guess you weren't. But it seemed like it was true then."

Progress. Small perhaps, but Laura was pleased. "You know how much I love you and your brother. I want you to be happy. That's what motivates me, sweetie. It's why I've done everything I have… always."

Kirsten stared down at the ground. Realizing she was embarrassed, Laura hugged her again. As she released her, Laura glanced toward the batting cage. Paul was watching her.

Chapter Eight

Paul currently owned two properties in Rosewood he had purchased to flip. One had been completed, the other he was ready to begin renovating. He had just listed the one that was finished and today was the open house. Laura's first one.

A midrange home, it wouldn't require anything on the scale of a gala, but he always provided a nice spread. Treating potential buyers like guests paid off.

He watched as Laura rearranged the dishes on the dining table. She had ordered a bouquet of tropical flowers—orchids, birds-of-paradise and some he didn't recognize. And there was a woody thing in it that looked artsy. Impressive. Laura had a touch with styling the table.

"The flowers are nice…unusual."

Laura angled her head, studying the arrangement. "The florist had to special order the exotics. But I think it makes the table." She had also brought some special serving pieces to supplement those the caterer provided.

"Table looks outstanding."

She smiled tentatively as she adjusted another dish. "You think so?"

"Might even be overkill. I've priced the place to sell fast."

"Then I'll consider it my practice run for the gala." She smoothed the sides of her skirt, even though it was in place.

"No need to be nervous. I expect to have some lookers and some serious buyers. And we only need one."

"Right." She clasped her hands together. "I'll just pretend I'm entertaining then."

"Hello." A prospect was strolling toward them.

"Welcome." Paul greeted the woman with a smile. "Help yourself to some refreshments and have a look around."

"Do you have a large family?" Laura asked the potential client.

"Two kids." The woman patted her stomach. "And another on the way."

"Then you'll love all the bedrooms and the huge family room," Laura enthused. "Not to mention three bathrooms."

The woman laughed. "Sounds great."

Laura poured her a cup of coffee, her hands shaking just a little. "Cream or sugar?"

"Both please."

Laura added them and stirred the drink. "Look around the house and if you have any questions, we're right here."

Smiling, the woman sipped her coffee. "I like the way you do business."

As she strolled deeper into the home, a couple entered. Paul watched as Laura spoke to them. Although shaky at first, her confidence grew as she talked with them. And with the next clients.

By the end of the day, the first woman returned with her husband and made an offer for a thousand over the asking price. It was a fair offer, and because the success of flipping depended on moving the property quickly, he accepted. He paid a daily interest for his short-term financing and each day the property went unsold cost him. This was an unqualified success.

And it was due in part to Laura. Despite her initial anxiety, she had spoken to the woman, answering all her questions, making her feel at ease. It seemed as though she might have the gift. Some Realtors possessed it. Others made their clients feel so uncomfortable, they rushed through a house without even seeing it. Since Laura hadn't passed her test yet, she had wisely given over the preparation of the earnest money contract to him. Still, she had sat by his side, watching how he did everything.

Locking up the house, she was still glowing. "That was great!"

"It's not always that easy," he warned. "And the buyers still have to qualify."

She shifted her briefcase. "Qualify?"

"Their financing has to be approved. Doesn't sound like that should be a problem, though." He checked the patio doors and clicked the lock in place.

She turned the lights off as they left the great room. "Is that why you took the backup offers?"

He nodded. "In case their deal falls through."

"I'm glad they were first to bid." Her heels clicked softly against the oak floor as they headed toward the kitchen.

"If theirs hadn't been the highest, it wouldn't be first in line." He tested the door that led to the garage. "You line up the offers by price first, then by the order they're placed. They happened to be first in making the bid and it was also the highest."

"I'd like to see them get it. They're so excited about the house." Laura adjusted the blinds on the window that looked out to the yard. "And they're a young family. They'll fill the place with love. I can just picture those toddlers playing out there."

"Clever of you to point it out to her."

"A fenced-in yard is a big inducement to parents. Saves a lot of worry." She sighed.

He picked up some brochures on the kitchen counter. "What's wrong?"

"Nothing. Just thinking about when Kirsten and Gregg were toddlers. Kirsten was so sweet, so loving."

"The teen years were definitely the toughest for my parents." He tucked the brochures in his briefcase.

Laura packed the coffee, sugar, creamer and cups back into the carton she had stowed under the counter. "I wish you'd known her when she was younger. No tantrums or bad temper."

"I like her now."

She smiled, her expression soft. "Thank you."

He thought about Gregg and Kirsten. "They're both well-grounded kids."

"That's why I brought them here," she said, reaching for the plastic spoons. "So they'll stay that way."

He studied her. "Bad influences in Houston?"

"You could say that. But that's behind us now." Laura repacked her personal serving plates. The caterer had already picked up his things. "Kirsten's softening, I think. She's going to the teen pizza party tonight. I'm hoping she'll make friends."

"You sound nervous." He wondered why.

"For her, not me. It's not easy being the new kid."

She wiped off a tray. "And she's taken Jerry's death really hard. They were close."

At least the kids had. More than could be said for her. "It's an impressionable age."

Laura shuddered. "I wouldn't turn the clock back to my teen years for anything."

"I'm sorry." He wasn't sure what else to say, yet he still wanted to know what it was in her past... maybe the secret she had alluded to.

Laura fiddled with the carton. "Nothing for you to be sorry about. It's just the way it was."

"Is that why you're not close to your mother?"

She concentrated on packing the remains of the refreshments. "Pretty much."

"Do you want to talk about it?"

"It was a lifetime ago. And talking about it won't change anything." She smiled with artificial brightness. "So, anyway, this open house was a success."

"Thanks to you."

"Really?"

"Yep." He picked up the cartons she'd packed. "No one would have guessed you're a first timer."

"Wow...Thanks."

"I just tell it like it is."

"Even so..." Her smile grew.

They passed through the dining room and he tipped the boxes in the direction of the table. "Why don't you grab the flowers? They'll just go to waste here."

"You don't want them?" She hesitated, her fingers tracing one silken petal.

"Do you like them?"

She touched the vase. "I did pick them out."

He shifted his load of boxes and briefcase. "Case closed."

They left by the front door, stowing away their cargo.

Paul retraced his steps to the front door, replacing the lockbox. "I'd better let you get home. I'm guessing you want to help Kirsten get ready for tonight."

She jerked her wrist forward to look at her watch. "Yipes. You're right." She headed toward her car, then turned to face him. "Um. If you're not doing anything, why don't you join us for dinner? It'll just be Gregg and me, of course, nothing special, just—"

"What time?"

"Around seven?"

"I'll be there."

Kirsten was all nerves as she dressed for the pizza party, changing her outfit several times. Ten minutes before it was time to leave, she was frantically searching for yet another.

"Sweetie, you look beautiful. Instead of changing your clothes again, why don't you pick out your accessories? I think your yellow bracelet would work. And maybe that cute new chain necklace?"

Kirsten looked torn. "You sure I look okay?"

"Absolutely."

Digging through her jewelry box, Kirsten pulled out the bracelet. But she chose another necklace. Then she put on the newest pair of shoes, the ones her grandmother had bought her just before they moved.

Tearing Kirsten away from the mirror, Laura finally steered her out the door. Kirsten was quiet as they drove to the church rec hall.

When they arrived, Laura took her hand. "Just be yourself. They can't help but like you."

Kirsten gave her a rare hug, then, embarrassed, scrambled from the car.

Gregg hopped into the front seat. "Girls are kinda goofy, huh, Mom?"

She laughed. "I don't know. I was a girl once, you know."

"I bet you weren't a goofy one."

"You're good for me. You know that?"

He fiddled with his iPod, a farewell gift from his grandparents. Laura shifted the car in gear. He was getting close to that age where she wouldn't be able to smother him in motherly compliments.

Back at the house, she started on the sauce and filling for the main dish and prepared a salad, which she topped with red grapes and pine nuts. Luckily, she'd made a three-layer coconut cake with orange filling the day before so dessert was taken care of.

Paul arrived promptly at seven. Gregg was happy to see him. Especially when Paul offered to toss a baseball until dinner was ready. It was the sort of evening she had always wanted for her family. But Jerry never had the patience for what he termed a waste of time. Instead he had shut himself in his study away from his family and any demands he thought they might put on him.

Laura grated fresh Caciocavallo and Parmigiano Reggiano to sprinkle on the pasta. The casserole was bubbling as she pulled it from the oven.

Oven mitts still on her hands, she called the guys in from the yard.

"I should have asked if you needed any help," Paul apologized after washing up.

"Everything's under control. It's a really simple meal. A pasta dish."

"Mom's is the best," Gregg told him.

Laura took the garlic bread from the oven. "Gregg's very loyal. I hope it's okay."

"Smells delicious," Paul replied.

After everyone was seated, Paul clasped his hands together. Belatedly, Laura realized he was accustomed to blessing the food.

"You're our guest. Would you say grace?" She hated to think she might stumble over the words.

Paul thanked the Lord for the food and the

company. He also asked Him to watch over the inhabitants of the house.

Laura swallowed an unexpected lump. When he finished, she covered by busying herself with pouring the iced tea.

"What kind of dressing is this?" Paul asked after a few bites of his salad.

"It doesn't have a name. It's just something I made up."

"I should have guessed it didn't come out of a bottle." He took another bite.

Pleased, Laura ducked her head. "Thanks. I like to experiment with my own recipes."

"She makes up cakes all the time," Gregg told him. "And other cool stuff for dinner."

Paul slid his fork beneath the remaining salad on his plate. "Nice having a chef for a mom."

"Yeah."

They ate quietly for a few minutes. Paul tasted his entree. Then took another bite of the tender chicken blended with fresh spinach and ricotta cheese. The filling was rolled in lasagna pasta and covered in a tangy marinara sauce. "This reminds me of Chicken Florentine. Your own recipe?"

She nodded. "It's similar. I call it my Florentine roll-ups. Gregg's my main taster, although Kirsten likes it, too."

"Did you ever consider a culinary career?"

She tried not to take his remark the wrong way. It didn't necessarily mean he was trying to divert her from the investment business. "No."

He winked at Gregg. "Your tasters have a soft job."

She relaxed. "I like experimenting with sauces. Cooking's a great way to get rid of stress."

"And more fun than exercise." He patted his midsection. "I'll be jogging this off in the morning, but it's worth it."

"You really like it then?"

"Don't tell the owners, since they're friends, but I like it better than most of what you get at the local Italian restaurant."

She blinked, then fiddled with her silverware.

He observed the motion. "Why?"

"Oh, nothing." Gregg was busy picking grapes from his salad. "Just that Jerry never cared for my cooking."

Paul paused, his fork in midair. "Really?"

"Afraid so."

"Maybe his taste buds were off."

By the time they had eaten dessert, which Paul complimented, as well, Gregg was getting antsy. "Can we practice some more?"

Paul looked at her.

"Fine by me if Paul doesn't mind."

"We should help with the dishes." Paul made a move to collect the plates.

"No. I'd rather you spend the time with Gregg.

It won't stay light forever. Besides, there's not much to clear."

Gregg jumped up and headed toward the door. "Come on, Paul."

"Shoo," she added.

From the kitchen window above the sink she could watch them. Paul was incredibly patient with her son. And he never raised his voice when Gregg made a mistake. She had cringed at the way Jerry had yelled at the kids. Strangely, they had worked that much harder for his approval. Not so strange, she reminded herself. She had done the same thing as a child.

It didn't take long to stack the dishwasher. With the food put away and the counters wiped down, she joined them in the backyard. She had picked up an old-fashioned swing at a yard sale. It was just the thing to pass a quiet evening in.

She loved old furniture, antiques. Probably because she felt disconnected from her own past, she supposed. But she could imagine the stories the old pieces held. So, she was gradually replacing some of her missing things with finds around Rosewood. Kirsten was horrified. Gregg didn't particularly care.

The light began to fade, twilight stealing the last of the day. When they could no longer see the ball, Gregg and Paul admitted defeat and retreated to the back porch. She had brought out glasses and a pitcher of fresh lemonade.

"I imagine you men need refreshment."

"Whew. Your son gave me quite a workout."

Gregg dropped onto the only chair on the porch other than the swing.

"Gregg, I think Paul would like to sit there."

He wiped his forehead. "I can sit on the swing, unless you mind?"

She scooted to one side, trying not to mind. "Of course not."

Paul lifted his glass in Gregg's direction. "You've got a strong arm. You keep practicing every day and you'll be quite a player."

Gregg grinned. "I want to be the pitcher next year."

"I was a pitcher way back when. I can work with you, if your mom doesn't mind."

Her smile was rueful. "We'd appreciate your help. I'm afraid I'm pretty hopeless when it comes to sports."

"You can't be an expert at everything."

"I'd be happy to cook for you in exchange for working with Gregg."

"It's not necessary."

The rebuff wasn't unexpected. But it still smarted.

She inched away from him on the gently rocking swing. Sipping their lemonade, they were silent as the moon climbed into the sky. And she wondered what a real family evening would have been like.

Chapter Nine

Paul entered the church sanctuary, and looked for the jacket he'd left there. The finance committee, which he chaired, had just finished their meeting. Rosewood Community Church had its challenges. Although it had a steady congregation, demands were always high. The school was constantly in the red and the food bank always needed bolstering. He had found creative methods to boost their bottom line, but it was always tricky.

The strains of a song filtered through the quiet building—choir practice. He stepped into a back pew so he could listen. To his astonishment, Laura stood in the front row of the choir loft.

He didn't know she could sing and he sure didn't know she'd joined the choir. He'd had business the past few days that had taken him to Dallas and she hadn't accompanied him.

The music director, Noah Brady, who was Grace's husband, tapped his baton. Although he was a busy surgeon, Noah always made time for the church choir. Grace accompanied the group on the piano. Despite scars from a massive car accident, her hands had healed well enough to play.

Paul leaned against the back of the pew in front of him. Of course not everyone in the group was talented. Noah held the philosophy that the Lord was pleased by all joyful noise. And he had a talent for blending the best and the worst, resulting in an even sound. Luckily, a few members were gifted.

As Noah had singled Laura out. Paul hoped she wouldn't be embarrassed. If anything would help her family, it was inclusion in church activities.

Then she opened her mouth to sing.

And he was amazed.

Her husky alto voice was vibrant, compelling. Then she reached for and found several high notes, and he realized that her range was incredible. The emotion she put into the song gave him goose bumps. Like a finely tuned instrument, she played her incredible voice, leaving a hush in the sanctuary when the last notes died away.

Then the singers all started talking at once. A rumble of compliments filled the choral loft as they crowded around her.

Paul had heard beautiful voices before, but

Laura's was magical. Yet, even from a distance, he could see she was blushing from the praise.

He sat quietly, waiting until the rehearsal was over. When everyone began leaving, he approached her.

"What are you doing here?" Laura said when she saw him.

"Listening to you."

She blushed deeper.

"You didn't tell me you could sing."

She shook her head. "I'm so out of practice."

He tried to see if she was putting on a show of false modesty. "It didn't sound like it."

She tugged at her hair, pushing a wayward strand behind her ear. "I haven't sung since high school."

"Why not?"

Laura shrugged. "No special reason."

What was she hiding? He felt it again, that sense of secrecy. "Weren't you in your church choir in Houston?"

She waved goodbye to Grace. "We didn't attend church."

"Never?" Suspicion flattened his voice.

She opened her purse. "No, I'm sorry to say we didn't."

"It's a new interest?" This didn't square with his picture of Jerry as a family man.

"Not exactly." She dug inside the purse looking for her keys. "Just that…"

Some of the choir members left down the main aisle, their voices trailing away as the door opened, then closed. "What?"

She slowed her search, raising her eyes to meet his. "Jerry didn't want to attend, and I didn't push."

Would she stand in the Lord's house and lie? "But you want to attend now?"

She resumed her search. "For a lot of reasons. Especially the children."

"If Jerry didn't want to go and you did, why didn't you take the children on your own?"

Disbelief flashed in her expression. "That wouldn't have been tolerated."

Tolerated?

She found her keys and clasped them tightly in one hand. "But I can now, so I've begun bringing the children. I understand it's never too late."

"Of course not…" But his mind was stuck on her choice of words. He couldn't process it. *Tolerated?*

"And everyone's been welcoming. Kirsten had a great time at the pizza party. She met some girls and really hit it off, and her friend from school, Mandy, attends this church. It gives them a bond. And Gregg…" She smiled indulgently. "He's already made a pack of friends, fun kids."

He watched her.

She closed her purse. "I love that so many of the people who grow up in Rosewood seem content to stay, and that so many generations of the same family remain connected."

It didn't jibe with her actions. "Yet you moved away from the children's grandparents."

Her expression sobered. "I had my reasons."

He shifted marginally closer. "The business?"

"Primarily." She took a half step back.

"What other reasons?" He wanted to know what she was hiding.

She tried to step back farther, but bumped into a pew. "I don't think you'd understand."

"Try me."

"The Mannings have some…control issues." Her knuckles turned white as she gripped the keys even tighter. "Ones I wasn't comfortable with."

"You mean about the kids?"

She nodded.

"I imagine they're pretty lost without Jerry." Even if she wasn't. "Don't you think they'd have pulled back once they found their footing again?"

"It's not that simple." She fiddled again with the sheaf of music. "It's just different now that I'm free to go where I want…"

Now that she was free?

She tucked her purse under her arm. "I should be getting home. Annie's watching the children and I don't want to impose."

He had the sense she was trying to escape. "**Why**

don't you bring Gregg to the park tomorrow afternoon? I'll help him with his pitch."

She shifted from one foot to the other, and he guessed she was weighing whether to turn down an offer that her son would appreciate. "We don't want to be an imposition."

"I wouldn't have offered if I didn't want to do it."

"Okay then. I appreciate the time you give to Gregg."

"A boy needs a man in his life. I was lucky. My father was there for me—in spite of any pain he was feeling."

"We'll see you tomorrow afternoon then. About six?"

"Tell Gregg to bring his glove."

"Will do. Good night."

Paul watched as she hurried to her car. It seemed that every nugget of information she revealed hinted that there was far more where it came from.

As the gala approached, Laura spent hours chasing details, confirming attendance of the symphony members and patrons. Because she had been so hands-on from the beginning with this particular house, Paul had also delegated the catering to her.

He listened to her suggestions for advertising on this one—making it an exclusive invitation-only event.

The well-heeled often preferred exclusivity. The house would sell itself, he knew, but the buyer would have to be someone with lots of disposable income.

This wasn't the first million-dollar-plus home he'd flipped. But they could be scary. The mortgage payments were huge. And they didn't stop until the place sold.

Laura was studying one of her dozens of lists. "If ten percent of the people we've invited show up, we'll be mobbed."

"Let's hope so."

She made a checkmark on her paper. "I rented a grand piano. It'll be delivered the day before the gala."

"Everyone else bringing their instruments?" He reached for the coffeepot. "We don't have to rent anything else?"

She continued checking her list. "Only a small ensemble will be playing and their instruments are portable."

He refilled her mug. "Don't worry so much about the details."

"Spoken like a man." She laid her pen down. "The art of making everything appear effortless is sweating every single detail beforehand."

"And you want it to appear effortless?"

"Then everyone will relax, enjoy the gala and the house."

He stirred some sugar into his coffee. "And buy it?"

"That's the plan, isn't it?" She added another piece of paper to her clipboard.

"In theory. But this house has a hefty price tag."

"Now who's worrying about details?" She reached for her coffee. "I really, really think the gala will sell the house."

He hoped so. Normally he wouldn't leave this much planning to a novice, but he wanted to test Laura. And he'd double-checked everything she'd done. "Construction should be finished just in the nick of time." He had decided to demolish walls in two rooms to make one larger area. The other renovations were moving along on schedule. He had some concerns about the landscaping, especially since they had added a waterfall in the back, but his man assured him it would be completed before the gala.

"Do you want to approve what I've ordered from the florist?" Laura asked, scanning yet another sheet of notes.

"Based on the last open house, you know more about flowers than I do."

She laughed. "You wouldn't say that if you saw the sorry state of my garden."

"What's the problem? Pests? Soil?"

She lifted her hands, palms upward. "I don't know. I don't have much experience in that area."

He frowned. "Your house in Houston had impressive gardens."

"Jerry hired professionals to take care of it. He thought what I'd plant would be too old-fashioned."

"I can take at a look at it, if you'd like." He slid open a drawer in the filing cabinet, then thumbed through the folders. "I'm no expert, but everything in my garden's in bloom."

"Tempting, but you're already doing so much for us...."

"Tossing a ball with Gregg?" He snorted. "Why don't I stop by after dinner, take a look around?"

"It does look pretty shabby...." She straightened her stack of papers. "You talked me into it."

Laura put away the remains of dinner. She had saved the double cream blueberry pie for later. If Paul was willing to work in her garden, she wanted to serve something more than cookies.

One of the bargain finds she had bought was a wrought iron and glass table. It suited the aged backyard. She had dressed it up with a cotton table-cloth, candles and her best dishes.

"Mom!" Kirsten called as she walked out of the back door. "Paul's here."

Since he was directly behind her daughter, Laura waved. His dog, Roddy, trotted next to him. The obedient animal looked happy to be with his master.

Paul was dressed in worn jeans and a T-shirt. The clothes accentuated his muscular build. It wasn't the first time she'd observed how attractive he was. But today he also seemed very male. Very immediate.

He held something in his hands. "My mother sent over some rose clippings she thought you might like."

"How…how very kind of her."

He showed her the thick stems. "They're strong climbers. They should look all right against the picket fence."

"I've always wanted a rose arbor," she confessed.

"It would be easy enough to build one. I probably have enough scrap wood in my garage."

"Oh! I didn't mean that as something else for you to do!" Embarrassed, she felt her cheeks flush.

"I enjoy working with my hands." He set down the clippings. "I don't get the opportunity much anymore."

Still, Laura didn't want to become indebted to him. "I appreciate your opinion on the garden."

"It's not difficult to learn." He walked over to a nearby circle of flowers and squatted down. Examining them, he rubbed a leaf between his thumb and finger. "See how this is yellowing? Needs iron. The right plant food has iron, phosphorus and bonemeal." He moved over. "These bugs on your columbine are aphids. They need to be sprayed—you can use an organic product."

Laura knelt beside him. "I didn't want to kill everything by doing the wrong thing. I don't own the place, after all."

"You just have to get in tune with the plants. It's like everything else in life."

He met her eyes and Laura felt her stomach flip. Realizing how close she was to him, she leaned back. But the feeling persisted.

"Where would you like me to plant the clippings?"

"Clippings?" she echoed.

"The *roses.*"

"Of course." Flustered, she stood to distance herself. "Um…by the fence like you suggested."

"I can bring more clippings another time when we get that arbor up." He unwrapped the tender stems.

"Oh." Along with her attraction to him, she felt a gust of fear. Jerry had controlled her for so long that she couldn't stand the thought of another man doing the same. And Paul was so strong it seemed it must be part of his nature.

"Is something wrong?"

"Wrong?"

"You suddenly went pale." He grasped her elbow. "Do you need to sit down?"

She pulled her arm back. "It's just a little warm."

"You're sure?"

"Yes." She shoved her hands into her pockets. "I'm fine."

"I've got some tools and fertilizer in the car. I'll

grab them and show you what to do with those clippings."

While he did, Laura went inside and began brewing some fresh tea. She needed to keep busy, to distract herself from the confusing thoughts he had caused. Who was he really? Another control freak like Jerry? After all, they had been best friends. Or, was he a considerate man? She had misread Jerry so badly she didn't trust herself to judge anyone else.

Gregg ran into the kitchen. "Mom?"

She took the ice trays from the freezer. "All through with your homework?"

"Uh-huh." His gaze lingered on the pie sitting on the counter. "What's Paul doing?"

"Getting some things out of his car to work in the yard."

"Can I help?"

She frowned as she dumped the trays. "Well, maybe. I don't want you messing with the bug spray, but you can probably do something else."

"Cool." He skidded out of the room, heading toward the driveway.

Kirsten opened the refrigerator. "Are we going to have pie soon?"

"In a little while. Would you put the sugar bowl on the outside table, please?"

Kirsten reached into the cupboard for it. "Would it be okay if Mandy comes over?"

"That sounds all right. It's a school night, so you can't stay up late, though."

"I know." She shifted the sugar bowl in her hands. "But I was thinking, could we have a sleep-over next weekend?"

Laura pulled the tea bags from the pitcher before the brew could get cloudy. "Just you and Mandy?"

"Maybe a couple other girls, too."

"I suppose so. My gala's at the end of the month and I'll want to clear the weekends just before it." Laura washed her hands. "We could rent some videos, order pizza for your sleepover."

"What about Gregg?"

"What about him?"

"You know, Mom." Kirsten followed her to the refrigerator. "I don't want him hanging around."

"I don't intend to tie him up for the night." She took a lemon from the produce drawer.

Kirsten started to protest.

"But I will try to keep him occupied and out of your way." Laura reached for a knife.

"Mom?"

"Yes, sweetie?"

"Do you like Paul?"

Laura cut the lemon into wedges. "He's a nice man and he's teaching me your father's business."

Kirsten toed her shoe against the tile floor. "No, I mean like a guy. He's around a lot."

"Paul was your father's friend. He thinks it's his responsibility to watch out for us."

"Maybe."

Uneasily Laura watched her daughter take the sugar outside. Was Paul spending too much time with them?

She found herself listening to his instructions on fertilizing and spraying for bugs as though on remote. She didn't do much better with the rose clippings.

"That's about it." Paul rested back on his heels. "We just do the same with the rest of the bed."

"Then I'll get us something to drink." Grateful for the reprieve, she headed inside. Charting his progress from the kitchen window, Laura waited until Paul was nearly done before she carried the iced tea and pie to the backyard. "Looks a lot better."

"They'll need to be watered every day." Paul dusted off the knees of his jeans.

She put the tray on the table. "I can handle that."

"Paul showed me how much water to put on," Gregg protested. "I can do it."

"I never turn down a helper. Now, how about some dessert and a cool drink?"

"That's something *I* never turn down," Paul replied. "What kind are we having?"

"Double cream blueberry."

"Is that different than regular blueberry?"

"I layer vanilla custard and sour cream on top of

the blueberries. And I add apples to the blueberries to give it a kick."

"Sounds great." He rubbed his hands together. "Can I wash up inside?"

She unloaded the tray. "Go ahead and take Gregg with you."

"Aw, Mom."

"Hands, mister." She chuckled, watching them. Paul teased the boy as they went inside and Gregg loved it. Paul was a natural, no doubt from having four siblings and an equal number of nieces and nephews. Her smile faded. Was Gregg getting too close to him? Would he expect him to always be around?

But when they came outside, Gregg was skipping, he was so happy. How could she take that away?

"The table looks all dressed up," Paul commented as he sat.

"It's something I like doing." She cut into the pie, serving him a hefty piece.

"I'm glad you're not stingy with portions." He picked up his fork. "I'm looking forward to this."

"I hope you still feel that way after you taste it," she fretted.

Kirsten dug into her own piece. "It's always the best."

Her daughter's compliments were rare, and Laura wanted to hug her. But she knew Kirsten would be embarrassed. "Thanks, sweetie."

"Mom makes everything the best," Gregg declared.

She did ruffle his hair. Then she filled the tea glasses. "Mint or lemon, Paul?"

"Um, mint I think." He crushed the leaf between his thumb and forefinger. "Can't get enough of that smell." He stirred his tea. "Or this pie."

The early-evening sun cast dappled shadows over the yard as the birds sang their last songs of the day. Laura enjoyed the quiet. She had felt at peace and safe here since they'd settled in. She had never felt that way at her home in Houston.

Both kids were developing an easy relationship with Paul. He laughed and joked with them. And despite Kirsten's questions about him, even she loosened up around Paul.

"So, Kirsten, how was the pizza party?" he was asking.

"It was okay."

"Just okay?"

"It was fun," she admitted.

"I bet the boys were glad you were there." He raised one eyebrow. "You meet anyone special?"

Kirsten blushed.

Laura looked at her closer. She hadn't been privy to this piece of news.

"Must have," Paul concluded. "You want to tell us?"

Kirsten fidgeted, then peeked at Laura. "His name is Brian. He's real cute."

Laura's eyes seemed to widen of their own volition. This was her baby. She seemed too young to be interested in boys. But she remembered being that age, the innocent crushes. And so she managed to smile. "I'm sure he is."

"It's no big deal," Kirsten assured her.

Oh, but it was. Especially the first case of puppy love. Laura could remember mooning over a boy in junior high who never looked her way. She had been devastated. "If you keep going to the church activities, I imagine you'll see more of him."

"Yeah." Kirsten's embarrassment seemed to be getting the best of her.

"More tea, sweetie?" Laura distracted her.

Grateful, Kirsten lifted her glass. "Sure."

"Kirsten's having a pajama party next weekend," Laura continued, knowing her daughter wanted to leave the subject of boys behind.

"Really?" Gregg asked.

Kirsten groaned.

"If your mother agrees, we could have a guys' night out," Paul suggested. "Go to the track, ride go-karts, play some video games, kill some hot dogs."

Gregg turned to her, bouncing in his seat. "Could I, Mom?"

Cornered, she smiled weakly. "Again, Paul, I think we're taking advantage."

"You kidding? Gregg and I'll have a great time. It takes a rare individual to appreciate hot dogs for dinner."

"Yeah, Mom, why not?" Kirsten chimed in.

Yeah, why not? Since she couldn't summon a valid argument, Laura capitulated. "Sounds like Gregg will have as much fun as Kirsten."

As Paul continued his easy banter, Laura found herself watching him. Instinctively, he had realized that Gregg would feel left out, and that Kirsten didn't want her little brother hanging around during this all-important first party in her new home. And he'd taken it on himself to fix the problem.

Chapter Ten

By the evening of the pajama party, Kirsten was alternately excited and racked with nerves. She double-checked all the snacks that Laura had bought or made. From the homemade dips, brownies and cookies to the selection of chips and sodas.

They had picked out the videos together, so Kirsten was happy with them. Laura guessed they would spend most of the time talking anyway. She hadn't been to many sleepovers as a kid, only to Donna's. Anyone else would expect a reciprocal invitation and she couldn't invite friends to her tumultuous home.

Paul arrived promptly to pick up Gregg.

"It's Paul!" Gregg hollered, running down the stairs to yank open the front door.

"Hey there! Got your running shoes on?"

Gregg looked down at his tennies.

Paul ruffled his hair. "Because we're going to be doing some moving."

Gregg grinned. "Cool!"

"I'm a go-kart fanatic," Paul confided.

"I think you've found a kindred spirit," Laura replied. "Gregg's been about to burst, looking forward to this."

"Me, too." Paul grinned at Gregg. "Us guys have to stick together, don't we?"

"Yeah!"

Laura straightened Gregg's cap. "Thanks again for doing this."

"My pleasure. Gregg, you ready to roll?"

"Uh-huh." He bobbed his head up and down and then bolted through the doorway.

Laura watched them as her son climbed into the Rover and Paul made sure he buckled up. Before she could reflect on them much longer, the girls Kirsten had invited started arriving. The house rapidly filled with giggles and sometimes hushed voices as they congregated first in the kitchen and then trooped upstairs to Kirsten's room. Although they had brought sleeping bags, Laura doubted there would be much actual sleep.

She picked up a few wayward purses and stowed them in the living room, smiling at the sounds from upstairs. She had been concerned about Kirsten's friends in Houston. She considered their values too superficial—they all attended the same exclusive private school and their parents belonged to the same country club. She knew there wasn't anything wrong with having money, but it seemed they spent more time discussing designer brands than anything else. These kids seemed more down-to-earth.

Laura put the plastic bottles of soda back in the refrigerator and wiped the counter. She knew that a new town wasn't a panacea for all their problems, but their new direction was promising. The influence of church was helping. These kids had all grown up attending on a regular basis so Kirsten didn't see it as geeky any longer.

As the evening progressed, the girls snacked and talked…and giggled more than either. Laura winced as the music got too loud, but it wasn't bad enough to bother any of the neighbors. And after a while they turned the CD player down, probably so they could talk more.

She made a fresh pot of coffee. As she reached for a mug, she heard a quiet knock at the front door.

When she opened it, Paul stood with Gregg asleep in his arms.

"Upstairs?" he whispered.

"Yes." She led the way to Gregg's room and turned down the bed.

Paul laid him down gently. Gregg barely stirred

when she slipped off his shoes. Covering him with a light blanket, she kissed his forehead.

Closing the door to his room, so the girls wouldn't disturb him, she said, "Thank you. He must have had a great time."

"He's quite the competitor." He kept his voice quiet, too. "I could barely hold my own with the go-karts."

"I just made some fresh coffee. Or is it too late for you?"

"I have some papers to look over so I won't be turning in for a while."

"Isn't it late to be working?" she asked as they walked back downstairs.

"I have an anxious investor. I want to work up some figures for him."

She took another mug from the cupboard. "Is it something I can help with?"

"No need."

After pouring the coffee, she remembered to take sugar to the table for his. "I can offer you brownies or cookies."

He rubbed his stomach. "We filled up on hot dogs *after* the go-karts."

She grinned. "Wise man."

"Experience. You feed kids and *then* take them on anything that whirls or twirls only once. So, how's the party going?"

"They've giggled most of the night."

"Unqualified success then. I don't imagine you'll get much sleep, though."

"I don't mind." She added cream to her coffee. "I'm relieved that Kirsten's making friends, settling in. It's been easier with Gregg, but Kirsten's been… more difficult."

"Isn't that pretty normal for thirteen-year-olds?"

"I suppose."

"Maybe you just need to give her time." He leaned back in his chair. "Things have a way of working themselves out."

She stirred her coffee. "I feel like I've spent a lot of my life just waiting…hoping things would change. In retrospect, I'm not sure that was smart."

"Why? What did you need to change?"

Automatically her defenses went up and she sipped her coffee rather than answer.

He pushed his chair back. "I'd better get going."

She felt a pang of disappointment. "Thanks again for taking Gregg tonight."

"I got the best of it."

"Oh?"

He grinned. "If you nod off, you could wind up with ice cubes in your pj's."

She laughed. "I'd forgotten about that."

"Or shaving cream in your slippers."

She winced. "You trying to make sure I don't fall asleep?"

"Worried?"

She opened the door. "Maybe I'll round up the girls and have them wrap your house in toilet paper."

"My nieces and nephews would be impressed. I hear it's a sign of being cool to have your house picked for that honor."

She leaned against the heavy oak door as he stepped outside. "I hate to crush your hopes, but don't plan on being cool."

"You really know how to wound a person."

She closed the door behind him. *No, that wasn't her speciality.*

The following weeks seemed to fly by as Laura was caught up in the preparations for Saturday's gala. She had talked Donna into joining them for the weekend since she was coming up anyway. The kids were excited about her visit, even Kirsten, who had been mellow since her party.

Friday night they ate dinner together, then talked. Kirsten volunteered to do the dishes as Laura and Donna caught up. The next day was going to be wild with last-minute details. Fortunately, the kids were going to Annie's for the gala's duration.

Once Gregg and Kirsten headed upstairs for bed, Laura leaned back in her chair. "I've really missed you."

"Me, too. But you're making friends here,

aren't you? Like this Annie who's taking care of the kids tomorrow?"

"She's great. I've met a lot of women I really like. But you know *me,* every ugly detail."

Donna frowned. "Why would you say that?"

"I can't tell these people the truth about Jerry." Laura propped her feet on the small ottoman. "It would make me sound like a horrible person."

Donna swirled the drops of condensation on her glass. "When you say 'people,' do you mean Paul?"

Laura drew her eyebrows together. "Why do you ask?"

"Because the kids talked about him all night." Donna's gaze was frank. "It's clear he's a big part of your lives."

"He's taken a real interest in them."

Donna watched her. "Just them?"

"You know why he's taken an interest in us." Laura crossed her ankles. "Because of Jerry."

"Sounds like Jerry's standing between you."

Laura shifted restlessly in the chair. "Like I said, how can I tell him the truth about his best friend?"

"You're sure he never knew?" Donna asked.

"I can't be absolutely sure...." Laura stared toward the window. Evening was ready to scuttle the last of the daylight. "But I think so. And I keep wondering how such different men ever became friends."

"Maybe Jerry changed."

"After he married me?" Laura didn't think so.

"You know that's not what I meant." Donna put her drink on a coaster. "But he could have changed in the years after they first met. Sometimes loyalty can blind a person to that."

"They met in freshman year at U.T. Both on the football team."

"I understand that's a real bond between men." Donna tapped the rim of her glass. "Maybe one that was too strong to see the truth."

"Even so…it's unlikely he wants to hear it now."

"Maybe," Donna mused.

"I'm not sure I like the way you said that…or the look in your eyes."

Donna waved her hand. "You worry too much."

Laura leaned forward. "And that makes me worry even more. You're not planning anything, are you?"

"Please! I'm just here to support your gala and celebrate your success."

"That's premature." Despite her reassurances to Paul about the easy sale of the "pink palace," she was worried.

"I don't think so. I trust your instincts." Donna sat back. "And I don't imagine Paul would have undertaken the project if he didn't believe in it."

"He knows exactly which properties to purchase and when." Laura reached for a pillow. "How much renovating they need to turn a reasonable profit, and he has an excellent network of investors to keep it happening."

"Well…"

Laura set her feet on the floor. "Well what?"

"That was said with pride."

Laura squirmed. "Shouldn't I be proud of my partner?"

Donna chuckled. "Sure."

She put the pillow behind her head. "That was said with a distinct lack of belief."

"I'm glad that you're so…fond of him."

"Donna!" She jerked forward, the pillow falling.

"Would you prefer to be on an unfriendly basis?"

Laura wagged her finger. "You're tricky. But you can stop reading anything into what I say. Paul doesn't see me in that light."

Donna crossed her legs. "You're sure?"

"I'm sure he was Jerry's friend. And that says everything." Laura stood, turning on another lamp. "You know…I wish I didn't feel this way, but I'm afraid that deep down he's like Jerry. Even his sister said he always has to be in control."

"That doesn't mean he would treat you the way Jerry did." She stood, too. "Are you maybe taking her words out of context?"

Laura remembered Jennifer's casual demeanor when she had said Paul had to be in control. Still…

Donna stretched.

"What are you thinking now?"

"That we'd better be off to bed because you've got an early morning and a huge day ahead of you."

"I am glad you're here, Donna. It'll help having a friendly face tomorrow."

"I'm on your side. You know that. But I have every confidence that you're going to shine. Even though Jerry criticized them, your parties were always perfect."

"Still…"

"He's gone now," Donna said gently. "Don't let him keep robbing you of your self-confidence. It's not fair to you or to the kids."

Laura hadn't thought about it that way. Was she really cheating her children by not getting over the past?

Everything looked perfect. Paul couldn't fault anything, from the floral arrangements to the catering. All of Laura's planning was paying off. Guests had begun arriving and they were raving about the music, the food and, most especially, the house.

Listening to his local real estate agent, he had listed the property at a price meant to move it fast. Although Paul had his broker's license he didn't concentrate his efforts on the sale. He left that to the experienced agents in each local area. His expertise was in locating and renovating the houses along with lining up investors. He knew when it was wise to delegate.

Looking around the successful party, he scratched his head. When he first met Laura, he couldn't have imagined her capable of pulling off something like this.

An ice sculpture glistened in the middle of the table, which held a sparkling crystal punch bowl. Incredible finger foods made an equally impressive display on an adjoining table. Laura had even thought to stock the pond with fish to entice the male visitors with visions of weekends relaxing in the country. And plenty of them commented on the wooden dock she had nagged him into adding, telling him it would pay for itself. Seemed she might be right about that, too.

He felt a hand on his arm and turned.

Allison, the interior decorator, angled her head, her heavily outlined lips curving in something between a smile and a pout. "I haven't gotten to say a word to you."

"Because you did your job well. Everyone's interested in the house, which is why I'm here."

"Of course." She waved toward the elaborate buffets. "No champagne fountain, Paul? I couldn't even find a glass of wine."

"I don't serve alcohol, but there's something most everyone should like—frozen specialty drinks, cokes, flavored teas, every kind of gourmet coffee drink I could think of."

"Aren't you worried you might offend your guests?"

"A lot of these people will be driving back to the city tonight. I don't want to cause any wrecks."

She sighed. "I suppose you're right. I just don't want to turn off any clients."

He smiled as he lifted his glass. "You should try one of these frozen things. I don't know what it's called, but it's tasty."

"Paul!" The Realtor waved him over to the other side of the room.

"Talk to you later, Allison." He could feel her eyes on him as he moved away. He hoped Laura wasn't right. But the warmth of Allison's glance had seemed more intimate than usual.

He answered a few questions about the remodeling, then circulated around the room. As he did he spotted Laura. She was smiling and chatting with some of their guests. Even though he knew how nervous she had been before everyone arrived, not much of it showed now. People seemed comfortable and plenty of them had roamed upstairs and around the grounds, checking out the property. He had held enough open houses to know this was a positive sign.

A few hours into the gala, he was fairly confident it had been a success. A quick word with the Realtor had confirmed that several people were ready to put in an offer.

When he saw Laura alone for a moment, he caught her attention. "I think we've done it."

She waited.

"Pulled this off—made it a success."

Her smile transformed her face. "You really think so?"

"The Realtor says we're looking at multiple offers."

She clapped her hands together silently. "Everyone seemed enthusiastic, but I was keeping my fingers crossed."

"All that planning made the difference."

Her cheeks flushed. "I really, really wanted this to be a success. I know you've put your trust in me and I didn't want to let you down."

"You're proving me wrong about not being able to handle the job."

Just then one of the caterers needed Laura. Paul watched as she deftly handled the situation, then turned to chat with more guests.

Laura's friend, Donna, waved to him.

"Enjoying yourself?" he asked, walking across the room to her.

"Everything's top-notch, but then that's what I'd expect from Laura."

He followed her gaze, watching Laura. She'd chosen a pale green dress made of some sort of floaty material. Her dark hair was wound up on her head and her earrings sparkled. He wondered if she had any that matched her eyes.

"She's looking better," Donna continued.

"Better?" He drew his attention from Laura to study her friend.

Donna sipped her punch. "Laura hasn't said anything, has she?"

"About?"

"Her marriage was difficult."

"Oh?" he questioned cautiously.

"She won't tell you this, so I'm going to. I know Jerry was your friend, but I don't think you really knew him."

Paul frowned at her bluntness.

"You're thinking I have a lot of cheek saying something like that."

He didn't say anything.

"But I've known Laura all her life. She had a raw deal with her parents, then an even worse one with Jerry. He was controlling, belittling and abusive. But she's never complained about it to anyone but me. I'm not saying she's a saint, just a good mother who didn't want her children to know the truth about their father. And that nearly ruined Kirsten."

He checked his annoyance. "Why are you telling me all this?"

"Because you're part of their lives. And I think

you ought to know the real Laura. The one underneath all that emotional abuse. You may think she's weak, but it takes a strong woman to protect her children, to take on the challenges she has."

"By that you mean me."

Donna looked at him evenly. "Yes. I just want her to get a square deal, not to be judged because of Jerry."

"You think I'd do that?"

"You were his friend. It's natural for you to be loyal, especially to his memory, because you can't confront him and ask for the truth. Why do you suppose Laura hasn't told you? Speaking ill of the dead isn't in her nature, despite what he did when he was alive."

Paul looked across the room again at Laura. He knew she kept secrets. But this…Had Jerry hidden a side of himself? Or did even the thought betray his memory?

Chapter Eleven

Laura was ecstatic about the results of the gala. They received several offers, which launched a bidding war. Paul accepted the highest—$2.4 million. They had purchased the property for $552,000. Even after their costs of $380,000 and a donation to the symphony of $100,000, they had made a tidy profit for the company and their investors.

And she had seen Paul's burgeoning respect for her. There was a lot riding on the success of this venture and she finally felt she was proving herself. Even the children seemed impressed.

She walked out to the car with Donna. "I wish you didn't have to go."

Donna popped open the trunk. "Me, too. But I have a meeting I can't postpone. I'll be back soon."

Laura hefted a bag into the trunk. "You promise?"

"Just try to keep me away." Donna hugged her, then wiped her eyes. "Now, see what you did?"

Laura wiped her own and laughed. Donna slid into the front seat, then waved as she drove off. Laura meandered through the yard, stopping to deadhead the rosebush. Her elderly neighbors strolled down the sidewalk. "Morning!"

"Hello there," the old gentleman replied, still holding his wife's hand.

They continued their slow journey and Laura let herself into the house. She had promised the kids they could start the memory book as soon as the gala was over. She dug into the closet, hauling out boxes of pictures and clippings. Then she took all the photo albums and scrapbooks from the bookcase. Settling on the couch, she opened the first box. Kirsten's first tooth. Gregg's first haircut. Jerry, kneeling in front of the Longhorn stadium, dressed in his uniform, holding a football. The pictures slipped through her fingers as she lost track of time.

"Mom!" Gregg skidded into the room, then dropped onto the sofa. "What'cha doing? Is this for the memory book?"

Kirsten followed more sedately. "Did you already start?"

Laura put a pile of loose pictures on the coffee table. "No. I gathered up what I could find, then started looking through them."

"Is this you and Dad?" Gregg held up one of the oldest pictures.

"That's just after we met." She took the photo and traced an outline of her smile. She had thought she had everything in the world to smile about.

As her children crowded close, Laura realized she did. Regardless of anything else, they were the richest blessings. Humming, she helped the kids lay out pictures from over the years.

When the doorbell rang later, she was still caught up in the past. Leaving the kids, who'd become just as absorbed as she had, she answered the door.

Paul stood on her front porch. "Hi. I thought Gregg might be able to come out and play."

She grinned. "That's a distinct possibility." Laura opened the door wider and he came inside. "Did you guys have plans I've forgotten?"

"No, just thought he might be up for some practice."

"We're sort of in the middle of something," she explained as she led him into the living room.

"If this is a bad time—"

"Actually, you might find it interesting. The kids are making memory books of their father."

This was the first mention of doing something to remember Jerry. High time.

Gregg insisted Paul sit beside him on the couch. "Look, here's a picture of Mom and Dad when they first met."

Paul picked up the picture. Laura and Jerry both looked happy. Under Gregg's direction, he looked at the other photos, as well. At first Laura seemed all smiles. But as the photos progressed in age, the strain in her smile grew. Many of the candid shots revealed an unhappy woman. Paul looked across the room at Laura. Sitting beside Kirsten, she was smiling more like the woman in the earlier pictures.

What was the real cause of her unhappiness? Donna's claims bothered him. But she was Laura's friend. She *would* put the blame on the one who couldn't defend himself.

Kirsten reached for one of the albums. "We're going to make a book for our grandparents."

"Great idea."

"It was Mom's," Kirsten acknowledged. "She saved all the articles from newspapers and Dad's sports stuff."

Laura squeezed her arm. "But Kirsten will be the one making it. And that will make her grandparents appreciate the book even more. Gregg's going to draw a picture for them, too."

Paul ruffled the boy's hair. "Good deal, pal."

"Grandpa puts my drawings on the 'frigerator like Mom does."

"You know why?"

Gregg shook his head.

"Because the kitchen is the heart of the home."

He picked up another photo. "That way your drawings stay closest to their hearts."

"Cool!"

Kirsten flipped through the pages. "Did you know my dad when you were little kids?"

"Afraid not. We met our first year in college." He put the photo down and reached for a scrapbook. "Most of the guys on the football team gave me a hard time because I came from a small town. But Jerry stood up for me. And he was a hotshot recruit from a big city. Because he did, the other guys backed off."

"My dad was the best." Kirsten sounded at once both fierce and sad.

"Yes." Paul saw the shadows in Laura's eyes.

She stroked Kirsten's blond hair. "This one was her daddy's girl."

Kirsten started flipping the pages again. "Nana and Grandpa are going to come for a visit soon."

Laura's smile froze. "They're coming in a few days."

"Do you have enough room? If not, I have plenty."

"Thanks, but they said they're making a hotel reservation, that they'd be more comfortable with their own accommodations."

"Still, it'll be good for them to see where you live."

She didn't look convinced. "They miss the kids."

Kirsten looked at her.

"And the kids miss them," Laura added.

"We'll have their book ready by then." Kirsten put the album on the coffee table.

"And my drawing," Gregg piped up.

"If they have time, I'd like to have you all over for dinner," Paul offered.

"Cool!" Gregg replied.

"It will be up to them." Laura shifted the boxes on the table. "But I can extend the invitation."

"And they can go to church with us," Gregg decided.

Paul could tell Laura didn't think that was going to happen.

"We'll see," she replied diplomatically.

Kirsten looked down at her hands.

"Kirsten, maybe if you invite your grandparents to church, they'll go," Paul said.

She shrugged. "Maybe."

"Right now we have to concentrate on the memory books." Laura handed her daughter a box of clippings. "Why don't you pick out the best ones?"

Paul could see that Laura was still worried. *Why?*

"They're here!" Kirsten hollered, ripping open the door and running outside.

Gregg was close behind her.

Laura waited until the kids quieted somewhat. Then she took a deep breath and went to greet her in-laws. "Edward, Meredith, good to see you."

Edward hugged her.

Meredith's smile was watery. "Laura."

Inside, they toured the house. Meredith withheld her comments until they were done. "Is this all? You don't have a separate family room?"

"We have all the room we need."

Meredith peered at the fluted columns on the fireplace that were so different from her own ultramodern home. "It's awfully old, isn't it?"

"Yes. It's Victorian." She pointed to the dentil molding that bordered the high ceiling of the living room. "I love the details."

Edward ran his hands over the back of a walnut rocking chair she had picked up in a yard sale. "You've made it real homey."

"Thank you, Edward." She mustered her courage. "We would have liked to have you stay with us."

He looked at his wife.

"We have more room at the hotel," Meredith hedged. Although Laura had suggested Annie's bed-and-breakfast, Meredith had chosen a hotel on the edge of town.

"And we're pretty uneven sleepers these days." Edward sat in the chair, launching into an easy rocking motion. "I get up half a dozen times in the night. We didn't want to disturb you or the kids."

"Well, we're just glad you're here."

Meredith looked as though she wasn't sure whether to believe her.

"I thought we'd eat out back," Laura told them. "It's such a pretty day."

Meredith peered at the dining room. "I don't suppose you really have enough space to dine inside."

"We have this neat table and stuff out back," Gregg told his grandmother.

"Gregg, why don't you show your grandparents around the yard while I make some lemonade?"

He took his grandmother's hand. "Okay, Mom."

As they headed outside, Laura prepared a pitcher of freshly squeezed lemonade and filled the glasses with ice. Everyone was seated around the table when she brought it out. "I hope you're hungry. I made Chicken Kiev for dinner."

"Oh." Meredith looked disappointed. "We had chicken last night."

Edward took a glass. "But not Kiev."

"No," Meredith admitted. "That's true."

"Mom's is really good," Kirsten told them.

Laura stopped pouring the lemonade mid-glass.

"I'm sure it is, dear," Meredith murmured.

"We stuffed mushrooms," Gregg said proudly.

"*You* did?" Meredith turned her attention to Laura. "Are you making the children cook?"

"They enjoy helping. Besides, they need to learn basic skills, to be self-sufficient."

Meredith frowned. "Jerry never learned to cook."

Edward held up his glass. "This is tasty. Did you make it yourself?"

"Yes. I squeeze the lemons, that's what makes it taste so fresh."

Gregg tugged at his sleeve. "I've been practicing my baseball, Grandpa."

"With your mom?"

"Sometimes. And sometimes with Paul."

Edward leaned back in his chair. "Is he your friend?"

Gregg bobbed his head in assent.

"Jerry's friend, Paul Russell," Laura explained.

"The one he appointed his executor," Edward said.

Laura passed the rolls. "As a matter of fact, he's hoping you'll have dinner with him while you're here."

"Oh." Meredith reached for her handkerchief, her eyes watering. "I would like to talk with him about Jerry."

"I'd like to visit with the young man, too," Edward interjected. "Good of him to invite us."

Edward was missing Jerry just as much as his wife. Possibly missing the boy he had been. But then, they hadn't seen the other side of their son. "Paul will be glad to hear that."

"Of course we want to spend most of our time with the children." Meredith put her arm around Kirsten.

"We're invited, too."

Meredith's hankie stilled. "Really?"

Laura felt uneasy. "He's taken a great interest in the children."

"I see."

From experience Laura knew that Meredith saw what she wanted to. "I'll go get the appetizers."

Although dinner wasn't exactly jolly, the kids were enjoying the visit with their grandparents. Even though Laura had never been able to develop a close relationship with Meredith, her in-laws were devoted to the children.

By the end of the evening, Laura was relieved when they left. They made plans to pick up the children the following morning, agreeing to be back in time for dinner at Paul's.

Laura was happy to let the kids go on their own with their grandparents. She wasn't sure she could have taken a whole day with them.

And they were back almost on time. Laura had warned Paul that they might be late, guessing Meredith wouldn't want to be told when to be back.

Laura hadn't been to Paul's home before and she wasn't sure what to expect. She was surprised to find that he lived in a century-old house, too. Unlike her folk Victorian, his was a Tudor revival. The steeply pitched roof and half-timbered facade could have come from a cozy English village. Inside, the house also incorporated the Craftsman qualities of exquisitely detailed doors and windows.

As he welcomed Jerry's parents, Laura looked around. His home reflected his sense of family. Yet it was all male.

Chocolate-colored leather couches and chairs were grouped around a massive open-grate fireplace and the imposing chimneypiece of carved stone was decorated with his family coat of arms. Pictures of his relatives were scattered around the living room.

She looked closer at the walnut molding. "I like your house."

"Funny thing. I took one look at it from the road and knew I wanted it. And for someone in real estate, that's not very smart."

She examined the molding's fine workmanship. "I can see why you did. It's charming."

Meredith was looking at her strangely, so Laura didn't say any more.

After Gregg petted the dog, he roamed around the room, looking at Paul's books and mementos. He didn't seem to mind. Gregg picked up a large picture frame. "I met these guys!"

Edward studied the picture. "You did?"

"At Paul's house. His mom and dad's one. They had a kids table I sat at."

"For dinner," Paul explained. "I think you remember how many brothers and sisters I have. Two are married now, with kids of their own."

"That's right," Edward mused. "I think Jerry would have liked having a bigger family like yours. But he was our only—"

They could all hear Meredith's sharp intake of breath. Then tears filled her eyes.

Edward paled.

Kirsten patted her grandmother's arm. "It's okay, Nana."

"I'll make you some tea." Paul headed toward the kitchen, Roddy following behind, his nails clicking on the wood floor.

"What's wrong with Nana?" Gregg asked in a loud whisper everyone could hear.

Laura smoothed the hair from his forehead. "She's missing your dad."

"Oh." Subdued, Gregg sat beside his mother.

The room was painfully quiet until Paul returned carrying a tray loaded with mugs. He offered the hot tea to Meredith and Edward. "I'm brewing some more for iced tea. Which would you like, Laura?"

She took a mug of the steaming tea.

"Kids?"

"Iced." Kirsten was definitive.

Her son was, too. "Do you have any Coke?"

"Gregg!" she scolded.

"He brought them to lunch that day," Gregg defended himself.

"Okay with you?" Paul asked Laura.

"I suppose so."

"Anyone else want a Coke?"

Kirsten raised her hand. "Me."

Laura refrained herself from lecturing the kids on their manners. Instead, she made sure Gregg didn't spill his drink.

"I hope everyone likes barbecue." Paul rubbed his hands together. "I'm cooking outside."

Meredith sipped her tea. "Seems to be common in this town."

Paul looked at Laura in question.

"We ate our dinner in the backyard last night," she explained.

"Glad everyone enjoys it. I've set up outside, too."

Laura bit back an unexpected smile. "Can I do anything to help?"

"Nope. There's a loin of pork on the barbecue. And everything else is made. I'll put some hot dogs on in a minute. Someone here seems to like them."

Gregg giggled. "That's me."

Edward nodded toward Kirsten. "I think someone else likes them, too."

Kirsten bobbed her head.

"Well, I do, too," Paul declared. "I'll put on several."

Edward added, "I haven't had a real hot dog in—"

Meredith cleared her throat.

"Like I said, I'll put on plenty," Paul told him. "I'm used to entertaining a lot of family and we're not very formal."

"Are you married, Paul?" Meredith asked.

"No." He perched on the arm of one couch. "It's just me."

"But I imagine you have a serious girlfriend," Meredith persisted.

"Afraid not."

Meredith frowned, then glanced at Laura.

"As I recall, you were a good friend to Jerry when you were in school together," Edward commented. "And then business, of course."

Paul got a faraway look in his eye. "He was the best friend I could have asked for."

Edward's Adam's apple bobbled as he tried to maintain his control. Laura laid a hand over his.

"I'm sorry I couldn't stay in town longer after… his services," Paul said. "If you'll remember, my sister, Jennifer, is expecting a baby and she'd been hospitalized that day. For a while, we thought she was going to lose the baby."

"Is she all right now?" Edward asked.

"Everything's fine, but we were pretty scared. That's why I had to get right back here."

"Of course," Edward sympathized. "And there wasn't anything you could do for Jerry then."

"I know you miss him."

Edward swallowed. "Every day."

Laura felt her heart constrict. For all that Jerry had hurt her, he was Edward's son, his little boy. She couldn't imagine losing Gregg.

As she thought about her son, he took the initiative and climbed into his grandfather's lap. Glancing at Meredith, Laura saw how alone she was. So she caught Kirsten's eye.

Understanding, Kirsten went to sit beside her grandmother. "Nana, are you going to church with us in the morning?"

"Church?"

"Uh-huh. My best friend, Mandy, goes there. And they have all kinds of stuff for us to do."

Meredith looked at Laura. "When did church become part of your agenda?"

"Shortly after we moved here. We'd really like it if you could join us."

"Can't you skip it?"

"We'd rather not."

"But we're only here for a short time," Meredith protested.

"I'm sure you'd enjoy meeting our new friends. Why don't you think about it?"

Meredith reached for her hankie. "You could be more considerate, Laura. After all, you're not only depriving us, you're depriving the children."

Laura's chin trembled.

"It wasn't enough that you dragged the children off to a strange town. We've barely set foot here—" she wiped her eyes "—and now you're making sure we can't see them."

"That's not—"

"Well, Laura, I knew when I lost my son that things would change." Her eyes watered. "I'd hate to imagine what he would think of your actions."

The kids, clearly unhappy, watched the adults.

"Kirsten, Gregg, could you guys give me a hand in the kitchen?" Paul asked. "Kirsten, you'll find the hot dog fixings in the refrigerator. Could you and Gregg carry them outside?"

"Sure." The kids quickly headed out.

Paul stood. "It might be better to have this conversation later, when the kids aren't around."

"Yes," Laura said gratefully.

"Well," Meredith sniffed.

Edward looked at his wife. "He's right."

"Could you stay an extra day?" Laura asked. "Maybe not leave until Tuesday?"

"We'll discuss it," Edward replied. "Since I've retired, I don't have a rigid schedule."

"Well, I have commitments," Meredith asserted.

"I'd appreciate it if you'd consider staying," Laura said quietly. "I know it would mean a great deal to the children."

The tension in the room escalated as Paul excused himself to check the grill. He wasn't sure what to think of Laura's relationship with her in-laws. To his way of thinking, they should all be pulling together after Jerry's passing. But he supposed death could fracture a family just as easily. Maybe the Mannings were afraid they were going to lose their grandchildren. If Laura remarried, she would have a new set of in-laws.

What was Laura afraid of? Her face was filled with strain.

Paul remembered Jerry saying that Edward was gone most of the time when he was a kid, working long hours to achieve business success. But Jerry had chosen to live near them as an adult so they must have become close. He reached for the hot dogs, then lined them up on the grill. Maybe Laura just hadn't tried hard enough to get along with the Mannings. She had been in an all-fired hurry to move away from them.

"Can I help?" Gregg asked, skidding to a stop after running out the back door, Roddy following close behind.

"Sure, pal. Open up the hot dog buns. We'll warm them on the grill."

Together, they watched the grill until dinner was ready to serve. He was sure getting attached to the little guy. He hoped that would have been all right with Jerry. His friend had missed out on so much. Kirsten might be at a difficult age, but they were both great kids. Kids who no longer had a father. And a mother he still wasn't sure about.

Chapter Twelve

The Russells didn't change their minds about attending church. They didn't exactly agree to stay longer, either.

Laura had stayed up late on Saturday night preparing several cold dishes so they could have lunch right after church. And she made a point of setting the dining room for the meal.

Paul had stopped by early that morning with a lush bouquet of roses for her table. He said they were a gift from his mother. Even so she was touched by the gesture. And the fragrance from the carefully cultivated flowers filled the room.

Using her best linen and dishes, Laura searched for any flaws in the preparation, but didn't see any.

"Mom, can't we change out of our Sunday clothes?" Gregg asked.

"I told you, I want you to look extra nice for Nana and Grandpa."

"They've seen me regular," he reasoned.

She grinned at his terminology. "I know, sweetie. But it's a special day."

Despite the constraints of his suit, he bounced about in his dress shoes. "Does that mean we can give them my drawing?"

"Yes."

Kirsten trailed her brother into the dining room. "And the memory book?"

"Sure, honey. They're going to be so pleased with it." Kirsten had been quieter than usual. Laura suspected it was the tug-of-war between her old and new lives. She smoothed the silky waves of hair that fell down her back. "Life can be confusing sometimes. Don't let it get you down, okay?"

Impulsively, Kirsten hugged her.

Laura kissed her forehead. "I'm proud of you, you know."

Kirsten drew back. "You are?"

"You've become a young lady…" Laura's throat filled. "A beautiful one."

Embarrassed, Kirsten walked to the refrigerator and pretended to study the contents.

The doorbell rang and Laura's nerves flew to attention. Maybe things would be better today.

Edward kissed her cheek upon entering. "Hello, Laura."

"It's good to see you both." Laura took his hat.

The kids rushed to greet them.

Meredith hugged them both, keeping her arm around Kirsten. "New dress?"

Kirsten tugged at the skirt. "We got it for church."

"Ah."

"Do you like it, Nana?"

Meredith sat beside her husband on the couch. "It's pretty."

Laura let out her breath. Things *were* going better.

"Nana, we have something special for you and Grandpa." Kirsten handed the memory book to her grandfather.

Edward was visibly moved as he turned the pages, lingering over pictures of a much-younger Jerry. Athletic and handsome, with his blond hair and blue eyes, he resembled a young Robert Redford. Meredith was uncharacteristically quiet as she looked through the book, tears filling her eyes.

And Laura felt her heart soften. Meredith wasn't her favorite person, but she had lost her only son, and Laura didn't doubt her love for him.

"It's very…thoughtful." Meredith looked so sad that Laura wished she knew how to comfort her.

"Yes," Edward agreed. "It was a wonderful idea, kids."

Kirsten perched on the arm of the couch. "It was Mom's idea."

Meredith appeared startled.

Edward looked up. "Kind of you, Laura."

She didn't want to shift their appreciation from the kids. Making the book had meant a lot to them. "The children really enjoyed making it for you."

"I did a drawing of our family!" Gregg announced, thrusting the paper into his grandmother's hands.

She studied it and frowned. "You've given your dad dark hair."

"That's not Dad. It's Paul," Gregg explained.

"Paul?" Meredith raised stricken eyes.

Uncomfortable, Laura tried to smooth over the moment. "He's spent time with the kids. And missing their dad, I'm sure Gregg—"

"It's clear what Gregg thinks." Meredith clutched her hankie. "You've already got another man moving in as Jerry's replacement."

Stunned, Laura shook her head. "You're misreading the situation. Paul was Jerry's friend."

"Do you think that makes it all right?" Meredith's voice could have withered the bravest soul.

Stung, Laura tried to explain. "Meredith, you're taking this all wrong. Paul is just—"

"I wondered why you moved here in such a hurry. It's obvious now. And Jerry barely dead. You should be ashamed."

Knowing the kids were listening to every word, Laura didn't remind her in-laws that it had been months since Jerry died. "I have nothing to be ashamed of. Paul has taken an interest in the children because he was Jerry's friend. And he's teaching me the business. That's all."

"I saw how he was looking at you yesterday," Meredith accused, her lips trembling. "I may be old, but I'm not blind."

Edward tried to calm her. "Now, dear, we don't-know—"

"*I* know. I know." She stood, her fingers white as she gripped her purse. "You'll regret this, Laura."

Feeling a chill of premonition, Laura stared at them. "I'm sorry you feel that way, but truly, you've got it all wrong."

Meredith's face was pale as she ran from the room, Edward trailing her. The children stared in silence as their grandparents left.

"What did she mean about Paul?" Gregg asked as the door closed behind them.

"Nothing, sweetie. Nana just got emotional thinking about your dad." She put her arm over his shoulders. "Don't worry about it."

"Then we can still see Paul?" he persisted.

Laura saw that Kirsten was studying her. "Nothing's changed, guys," Laura said.

But as she picked up her son's drawing, she

wondered. Gregg had drawn them as a family. With Paul standing shoulder to shoulder with her.

Laura called the hotel the next day, checking to see if her in-laws were still in town. They were still registered, but didn't answer the phone, so she left a message.

Hoping Meredith had a change of heart, she didn't go to work, having explained some of the situation to Paul. By evening, though, she hadn't heard from them. The kids were disappointed, but she really didn't know what to tell them.

After dinner she wandered in the backyard, too restless to settle down. The kids were doing their homework upstairs. She heard the gate creak and saw Paul.

"Hope I'm not interrupting," he began. "Are your in-laws here?"

She shook her head.

"They still in a tiff?"

"I'm afraid so."

He held another bouquet of roses. "I brought these for Meredith. They're from my garden. I thought they might thaw her a little."

Laura hadn't told him the cause of their argument, preferring to not embarrass either of them. She had simply said her in-laws were unhappy with her. "It's a nice thought, but I think it's going to take more than flowers."

He extended the roses. "How about you?"

She accepted them, bending to sniff the plump blooms. "They're lovely."

"Do you want to tell me about the argument?"

She bit her lip. "Not really. I hope you don't mind, but—"

"Enough said. Just thought you might want a sympathetic ear."

"Sympathetic?"

"Seems like you need one."

"Really?" She could use an ally.

"I've been thinking about Jerry…and that maybe people do change."

"After he married me?" she said, hopelessly.

"I didn't say that."

She had to ask. "But you think so?"

"I'm just trying to make sense of this, Laura. Donna gave me such a different picture of Jerry…"

"Donna?"

"She's just looking out for you."

Laura touched the velvety petals of the roses. "And are you making any sense of it?"

Paul met her eyes and she felt herself tremble.

He hesitated. "You've surprised me…in a lot of ways."

She heard someone harrumph.

Startled, Laura turned toward the house. And saw her in-laws standing on the back porch.

Realizing the picture she and Paul made as they stood in the shadows…as she held the bouquet of flowers… Laura groaned under her breath.

She hurried toward them, Paul following.

"Meredith, Edward, it's not—"

"I've seen quite enough, Laura." Meredith's voice shook, her face pale.

"Actually Paul brought the flowers for you," she explained, holding out the bouquet. "He thought you'd be here."

"I'm no fool." She gripped her purse. "I thought better of you. Why did you have to do this?"

"Meredith, please…" Laura followed her mother-in-law, who cried as she rushed back into the house, toward the front door. "Edward?"

He put his arm around his wife's shaking shoulders as they left.

The kids stared, eyes wide.

Sickened, Laura watched her in-laws leave, then turned to her children. "We'll talk about this later. Why don't you finish your homework now?"

"Okay, Mom." Gregg replied, heading back upstairs.

Kirsten studied her a few moments longer but didn't say anything as she followed.

"I'm sorry, Paul. I'm afraid my mother-in-law's

gotten hold of the wrong idea and she just doesn't want to let go."

"That's what the argument yesterday was about?" Miserably, Laura nodded.

"It'll blow over. When she sees there's nothing to her suspicions."

Laura dredged up a smile. "I think I'd better talk to the kids."

As she closed the door behind him, the last wisps of hope disappeared.

Paul rattled around his office, picking up an abstract, then finding himself so distracted he couldn't study it. Pencil poised in midair, he tried to concentrate.

Jerry hadn't just been his fraternity brother, he had thought of him like a real brother. Then he remembered the photographic history of Jerry and Laura. Had something else caused her unhappiness? Not the children. Clearly she adored them, despite Kristen's teenage tantrums. Her own past? Her estrangement from her family? Possibly.

The door opened and Laura breezed in. "Sorry I'm late. I was hoping to hear from Meredith and Edward."

"They haven't called?"

"No." She stowed her briefcase under the desk that was now distinctly hers. "And it's funny because they're still registered at the hotel."

"The kids okay?"

"I explained things to them. Gregg's fine." She flipped open her planner. "Kirsten's…well, she's having a little more difficulty."

He hated to see the kids hurt by a misunderstanding. "You want me to talk to her?"

"It might help. She likes you. She's just worried about her father being forgotten."

He met Laura's eyes. "That's not likely."

She abruptly looked away. "No, it's not."

He stiffened. Just the smallest mention of Jerry…How could she have been married to him and not feel a twinge of the grief he did? He let the silence build between them. But one of the drawbacks of a small office was the proximity.

She sighed.

"Did you go by the hotel? See if you could catch your in-laws?" He opened the middle drawer in his desk and rummaged around. "Maybe they've had a change of heart."

"I think you're overly optimistic."

"My mother's fault." *The one who had asked him to give Laura more time, to get to know her.* "She always said she refused to raise any pessimists."

Laura smiled. "No wonder I like her."

He found the pencil he'd been looking for. "That reminds me. She wants you and the kids to come to dinner one night this week."

"We'd like that." It certainly sounded better than chasing down the Mannings. Laura didn't want to see her mother-in-law, but she needed to mend this rift in the family. "I guess I should go by the hotel, find out if they'll talk to me."

He opened a folder. "Okay."

"Unless you need me here?" she asked hopefully.

"I've got everything under control."

"Of course." Reluctantly, she picked up her purse, then took more time than necessary to locate her keys.

Paul didn't look up from the file he was studying. "Stalling won't make the problem go away."

Caught out, she finally left. But she drove ten miles under the speed limit until she reached the hotel. And then she sat in the car for several minutes before she found the courage to go inside. She wished she didn't have to see her in-laws—she hated confrontation. But she knew she couldn't sit in the car all day, either.

When she entered the hotel lobby, she spotted them immediately. They were sitting with a man Laura didn't recognize.

Edward rose when he saw her. "Laura, come join us."

The man with him got up as well, extending his hand. "Duane Echols, Mrs. Manning. Echols Realty. You may have heard of us. Our office is just off the highway."

She nodded. Why were her in-laws meeting with a local Realtor?

Meredith didn't make her wonder long. "We've just rented a house in town."

"Here?" Laura asked stupidly. "In Rosewood?"

"Yes." Meredith reached for the hankie that hadn't been out of sight since Jerry died. "We realize you need help raising the children."

Laura felt her throat close. Stifled, she couldn't seem to breathe. For a moment she wondered if this was how a drowning person felt.

"That's mighty generous of you." Duane nodded, a fervent motion that didn't do anything to stir his stiff, sprayed gray hair. "If more people felt that way, families would be better off."

"Family comes first with us." Meredith dabbed the hankie at her moist eyes. "And Jerry's children are all we have left of him."

Apparently so, since she didn't count, Laura gathered. "But you've only been here a few days…"

"That's how long it took you," Meredith countered.

"Where…where is the house?"

"Two blocks from yours."

Laura felt the walls closing in around her. She had signed a year's lease and couldn't break it. "When… when do you plan to move?"

"Immediately." Meredith tucked her hankie into her bag.

"As soon as we can wrap things up in Houston," Edward added.

"Are you...are you selling your house there?" Laura asked in a faint voice.

"Not yet," Edward replied. "We'll have to see how things go here."

It was a tiny sliver of hope, but Laura held on to it.

Meredith stood. "Now, I suggest we get on with our arrangements, Edward."

"Nice folks," Duane proclaimed. "I bet you're going to be happy having them here."

As he hurried to catch up with the Mannings, Laura stared in numb silence. When she found her voice it was a mere mutter, and then only to herself. "There's not enough optimism in the world to believe that."

Chapter Thirteen

Paul squirmed in the armchair once Laura and Gregg had discreetly left him alone in the living room with Kirsten. He regretted his hasty offer to talk to the girl after Laura, shell-shocked, had returned to the office the previous day. Personally, he thought the Mannings would turn out to be a lot of help, even though Laura acted as though they were bringing the plague with them.

Kirsten sat across from him, staring so soberly he felt as if his collar was tightening on him where he sat.

"Your mom tells me you're worried everyone will forget your dad."

If anything, her expression grew even more intense. "Mom shouldn't be thinking about...well, anyone but him."

"I think about him, you know, all the time."

She studied him suspiciously. "You do?"

"It's hard for me to believe he can be gone." They'd been so young when they'd met. "Sometimes I wake up and for a few minutes I think he's still with us."

She looked down at her shoes. "Yeah, me, too."

He leaned forward. "Then it's pretty rotten when I remember."

Her lips trembled and he could tell she was holding back her tears. "Yeah."

"But your dad wouldn't want us to be sad. And he wouldn't want any of us to stop living and having new experiences. That includes your mom."

"Are you in love with her?" Kirsten asked.

His thoughts spun. Where had this come from? He admitted Laura was more attractive now that she didn't look like a whipped dog…But love? He had sworn off it. "We're just getting to know each other."

Her eyes narrowed. "Sounds like something grown-ups say when they don't want to give the real answer."

Paul frowned, realizing this talk had really been a bad idea. "Kirsten, I care about your family…you and Gregg…and your mom. I want to make life easier for you. It's something I promised your dad. Someday your mom may find someone else to love." *Why was that thought so unsettling?* "But that won't change how she feels about you."

She considered this. "But you don't want to marry Mom?"

He was in so far over his head he couldn't see daylight. "That's kind of premature, don't you think?"

She shifted restlessly. "My friends in Houston have divorced parents who got married again right away."

"Your mom and dad didn't divorce."

Kirsten appeared torn between sadness and anger. "Mom wasn't happy."

That wasn't exactly a surprise. "She's trying to give you all the best opportunities. Don't you want the same for her?"

She frowned. "What do you mean?"

"If she wasn't happy, don't you think she deserves a chance to be now?" *Was that really true?*

"What about us?" The child in her resurfaced.

He thought about Laura's interaction with her children. "Your mother will never be happy unless you and Gregg are, too. So, are we okay?"

She shrugged. "I guess so."

"Great." He stood, relieved the talk was over.

She left to join her mother and brother out back. Paul followed slowly, pausing at the open French doors, watching Laura with her children. She laughed, her face lit up. Had she changed that much? Or was he beginning to doubt Jerry?

It took less than two weeks for Meredith to entice the kids to come to her house without permission, frustrating Laura. Although the kids now had friends and activities in Rosewood, they weren't immune to gifts. And Meredith was handing them out as if every day was Christmas.

She was relieved to be at the Russells. That night Elizabeth had included Laura and her children in a midweek dinner. It was casual, uncomplicated. Like the company. Laura had thought some of Paul's siblings might be there, but it was a small gathering. Although she enjoyed his entire family, she savored this time alone with his parents.

"Paul's always been the independent one, the leader," Charles mused, watching his son toss a baseball with Gregg and Kirsten. "And I don't think it's just because he's the oldest. He did have to pitch in a lot when he was a kid because of my injuries."

"That must have been a difficult time for you," she said quietly.

"Only because it made things so hard for my family. I'm no saint. But the pain was temporary and I knew it." He squeezed his wife's hand. "Elizabeth helped me get through it. That, and I knew the Lord was watching out for me."

Laura swallowed. Such honest, raw faith. And it must have taken so much for him to get through all he had suffered.

"We're very blessed…with our children and grandchildren." Elizabeth patted Laura's arm. "And their friends."

"You've been very welcoming to us." Laura's voice caught.

"Because we like you," Elizabeth responded.

"And the kids," Charles added. "Think I'll join them." He was stiff rising and his gait was halting, but he was all smiles as he picked up a glove and joined the game.

Gregg ran and picked up any balls he missed, returning them without any fuss.

"The kids are well-grounded," Elizabeth said as she refilled their glasses with lemonade.

Laura couldn't hide her pride. "I think so. Paul's a natural with them."

"He's getting attached to them."

Laura looked across the yard. "You think so?"

"Surely you see it?"

Was that a good thing? Or would he try to assert his control over them? "I didn't want to read too much into it."

"And I didn't mean to sound nosy."

"But you're not! Nosy is more like…" Laura stopped.

"Paul's told me about the Mannings," Elizabeth said. Embarrassed, Laura ducked her head.

"There's no need to be embarrassed. As much as I love my mother-in-law, I used to be intimidated by her. She was so capable and knew everything. It made me feel totally inadequate. But then she sat me down and told me she had once been a young, nervous bride, too. She said that I shouldn't be threatened, that her role was to remind her son to always respect, love and treat his wife with kindness. And that, difficult as it was to imagine, one day I'd be a mother-in-law, too." Elizabeth laughed. "It seemed impossible at that time. I'd barely married Charles. But, of course, she was right and now I am. Just like you will be one day. Maybe, if you try to view your mother-in-law like you would any other woman, you'll understand she has weaknesses and foibles, but that she loved Jerry as much as you love Gregg."

Charles hollered a heads-up at Gregg who ran to catch an overthrown ball. Paul cheered when he caught the high fly.

"If you try to deal with her as a person, rather than a figure," Elizabeth continued, "it may be easier to understand that this is a natural cycle of life. How we handle our own mothers-in-law…well, it could determine how successful our relationships with our children's spouses will be."

Laura hadn't thought about it that way. But she knew Elizabeth was right. Meredith had loved Jerry with all her heart. And despite her manipulation, that heart was now broken.

"Have you read the story of Ruth?" Elizabeth asked.

"It's been years since I read my Bible," Laura confessed.

"Ruth is widowed, left alone with only her mother-in-law. By the law of that time, she didn't have any responsibility for her late husband's mother, but she took it on herself, working hard to support them both. She made sure her mother-in-law retained her dignity, and her grace has inspired women for centuries."

"It sounds like a story I need to read."

"Please don't think I'm being critical." Elizabeth patted her arm. "I'd like to be here for you, if you need it. In addition to wrinkles and graying hair, age has the benefit of experience."

Laura's eyes stung with unexpected tears.

Elizabeth pulled her into a hug. "How would you like me to invite Mrs. Manning for lunch? The three of us could talk, get to know one another."

Laura wiped her eyes. "It probably wouldn't be much fun for you."

"Helping you will be a pleasure." Elizabeth looked across the yard at her son, who threw the baseball to Kirsten. "I've sensed that you've gone it alone for a long time."

Somehow Elizabeth had guessed how unhappy her marriage had been. Instead of being embarrassed, Laura felt relieved. This incredible woman had offered her a shoulder to lean on.

* * *

True to her word, Elizabeth planned a luncheon for the three of them at her home, telling Laura she thought the informality would be more effective than a restaurant.

Meredith wore a loose-fitting pale gray, linen suit that emphasized her thin frame. Laura hadn't noticed before that her mother-in-law must have lost weight recently. From grief no doubt. Laura hoped this lunch might start them on a journey of reconciliation. They both needed it.

Elizabeth dressed her dining room to perfection. From the starched linen to the crystal and antique silver. Any informality meant location only, not the lunch itself. They started with an exquisite lobster bisque, followed by incredible seafood crepes.

"This is remarkable." Meredith touched her napkin discreetly to her lips. "The crepes are especially delicious."

Elizabeth nodded. "It's an old favorite. My mother liked to serve them at DRT meetings."

"DRT?" Meredith asked with a lifted brow.

"Daughters of the Republic of Texas."

"Oh, I know what it is." Meredith stared at her hostess. "Are you saying you're a member?"

"You could say it's a family tradition." Elizabeth refilled their water glasses. "The cousins who founded it are relations on my mother's side."

Meredith's eyes widened. "It's an impressive organization."

And extremely difficult to join. A prospective member had to prove lineage to one of the founders of the Lone Star state. In Texas, it was more impressive than being a member of the Daughters of the American Republic. And, it was a status Meredith hadn't been able to achieve. Laura reached for the cream.

"Occasionally, we invite visitors to the meetings." Elizabeth poured more coffee into Meredith's cup. "Perhaps you'd like to join us."

Meredith laid her napkin down, clearly taken aback. "I'd love that."

"Why don't we have our dessert in the conservatory?" Elizabeth suggested. "It's more comfortable."

"Dessert?" Meredith started to shake her head. "I'm rather full—"

Elizabeth pushed her chair back. "It's a light pear *glacé.*"

Once again, the perfect choice.

The airy room was filled with wicker furniture covered in plump cushions and green and blooming plants.

There were photo albums on the glass coffee table. What was Elizabeth up to?

Elizabeth brought in a tray with the dessert. "Meredith, I'm pleased to have found some pictures of our boys from their fraternity and football days."

Treat her as you would any other woman, as a person.

Laura had planned to sit in a chair. Instead she took the spot next to her mother-in-law on the love seat. "I'd enjoy seeing them."

Meredith allowed her uncertainty to show for a moment. "Whatever you'd like."

Elizabeth offered one of the albums to her. "I never tire of looking at pictures of my children."

"I wish I'd taken more," Meredith acknowledged. "It always seemed there would be plenty of time…."

"The Mannings have some lovely family portraits," Laura told Elizabeth.

Elizabeth opened another album. "Most of ours are casual snaps. The larger the family grows, the harder it is to get everyone together."

Meredith was studying the photos, caressing Jerry's face in one.

Laura's heart ached. She couldn't imagine losing one of her children. And without anyone else she was close to, Meredith must feel terribly alone. Edward, too, since their connection to each other wasn't strong. "Jerry was the captain of the football team," Laura told Elizabeth. "He could have gone pro if he'd wanted."

"You both must have been proud of him."

"Yes," Laura answered truthfully. At the time he had been her hero.

Elizabeth looked up from the album. "Paul was always grateful for Jerry's friendship."

It was difficult to read Meredith's reaction. She continued looking at the album in her lap.

Laura hoped it was a start.

Chapter Fourteen

Paul had set up dozens of folding chairs on the church lawn. Along with the other volunteers, he had begun by putting up the long tables first. For the church picnic, some people would bring quilts or blankets and spread them out on the soft grass. But the older folks mostly preferred chairs to sitting on the ground.

He wiped his forehead. The day was warm, and the skies were clear. From the amount of people already arriving to load the tables with their homemade contributions, it looked as though they would have a respectable turnout.

He spotted his sister Jennifer. Her husband, Alec, carried a large Tupperware bowl with one hand and held on to their toddler with the other. Jen seemed to be walking more slowly than usual, but then her pregnancy was advancing.

"Hey there."

"Hey, yourself." She rubbed the small of her back.

"Are you okay?" He didn't like the puffiness in her face.

"Just pregnant." She eyed the chairs. "But I think I'll take one of those before they fill up."

"You want a pillow? For your back?" He knew he could find one in the nursery.

She waved her hands. "Don't make a fuss."

It *was* a warm day. Maybe that's why she looked so tired.

"Would you mind seeing if Alec needs help with the kids?" She stretched out her legs, crossing her swollen ankles.

"Sure. Holler if you need anything."

She rested her head in her hands. "All I need is a few minutes here in the shade."

Paul hoped so. She'd already had one scare during this pregnancy. He caught up with his brother-in-law. "Jen's resting."

"It's about time." Alec gripped the hand of his six-year-old daughter, Lexi. "She's been running like there's no tomorrow. And the doctor told her to take it easy."

Paul had looked out for his family his entire life. It had given him a second sense about all his siblings. "Did she sleep okay last night?"

Alec looked worried. "She was up and down all night. Said it was just her back, but I don't know."

Paul stared across the lawn. "And you couldn't talk her out of coming today."

"Nope." He let go of Lexi and jiggled the toddler on his hip. "Said we all needed an outing."

Thinking of everyone but herself. That had always been Jen's way. "We can gang up on her. What do you think?"

"She'll be the most difficult about games with the kids." Alec watched as Lexi spotted one of her friends and ran to join her. "If you want to be Lexi's partner, I can take the baby and look out for Jen."

Paul had to remind himself that his siblings were all adults now. Jen, next in age to him, had always been special, had been his baby sister the longest. But she had a husband. And Paul knew he had to follow Alec's lead. "Sounds like a deal. Besides I haven't nearly killed myself in a three-legged race in a long time."

But Alec didn't laugh. His attention was on his wife.

Paul reached out for little Toby. "Why don't you check on Jen? The Tobester and I can find something else to do."

"Thanks." Alec handed off his child and hurried across the lawn.

"So, Toby, what do you have to say for yourself?"

The boy laughed, revealing nearly toothless gums and enough drool to promise more teeth were on the way.

"A teething biscuit, you say?" Paul chucked Toby under his numerous chins. "I bet your Aunt Robin has some with her."

"He can't talk, can he?" Gregg asked, startling him.

"Not yet, but we communicate anyway." Paul looked for Laura, saw that she was putting something on one of the food tables. "Where's your sister?"

Gregg pointed to one side. "With Mandy. They're always together."

"From what I remember about my sisters at that age, they were pretty much glued to their best friends. And when they weren't together, they were on the phone."

"Yeah." Gregg crossed his eyes. "They're silly."

Paul laughed. "We have to face it. Girls are just different."

Gregg made a face. "*Way* different."

"Some are okay, though." He had several in his family that were top-notch, including the niece he kept a watchful eye on.

"My mom is," Gregg agreed. "She's not silly. She does fun stuff."

Intrigued, Paul leaned closer. "She does?"

"Yeah. All the time." Gregg wiggled the baby's toe, making Toby laugh. "She makes stuff for my class, and takes us to movies, the park…the zoo."

"The zoo?" Rosewood didn't have a zoo. "You mean in Houston?"

"Uh-huh. It's a cool zoo with a train that goes around it." His eyes shone. "You go by the pond with ducks and through a tunnel. Me and Kirsten and Mom would ride it a bunch of times."

Paul shifted Toby. "Oh, after your dad…passed away."

Gregg shook his head. "Uh-uh. Before."

Paul didn't want to upset the child, but knew he should feel free to talk about his father. "So your dad was with you at the zoo, too?"

Gregg stubbed the tip of his tennis shoe into the grass. "He didn't like stuff like that. Mom always took us."

"Not everyone likes the zoo." Paul felt uneasy in the pit of his stomach.

"Dad didn't like the other stuff, either." Gregg shrugged. "He was busy, so Mom always took us places, and came to school stuff."

Paul didn't like the picture that was forming. "But you had barbecues and parties at your house?"

"For the grown-ups."

Paul's stomach felt as if he'd eaten a boulder. "I bet you saw a lot of your dad when you went on vacations."

"Dad said we weren't old enough to 'preciate trips. And he played golf on Saturdays and Sundays so there wasn't enough time to go anyway."

Paul held Toby closer, thinking it was Gregg

who needed the extra attention. Why hadn't Jerry spent more time with his children? Was Gregg's view skewed? "I bet there was time to go on picnics, though."

"Mom always puts surprises in the bottom of the picnic basket."

Where was Jerry in this family picture? Had Laura made it difficult for him to be part of his own children's lives? Or was it Jerry's choice? Donna had said: *I know Jerry was your friend, but I don't think you really knew him.* And she had claimed that Laura had been a victim of emotional abuse. It had seemed like a convenient excuse for a woman who wasn't satisfied with her husband. Was he letting his loyalty blind himself to the truth?

Laura approached, her smile tentative. She still had a timid way about her, but not nearly as much as when she had first moved to Rosewood. Working with her day in and out, could he have missed the subtle transformation?

"Hello there," she directed her words to Toby, who returned her smile with a pink gummy one of his own. "Is this cutie yours for today?"

"Just for a while." He watched as Laura chucked the dimples in Toby's plump knees. "Then I'm partnering with Lexi for the games."

Gregg rocked back and forth on his tennies. "Me and Mom are doing the races, too."

Laura groaned. "And I'm not the world's fastest land animal, but Gregg says that's okay." She laid an arm over the boy's shoulders.

"Winning isn't everything." Paul watched the interaction between mother and son.

"Sure, easy for you to say. I'm not athletic." She ruffled Gregg's hair. "Fortunately my partner is."

Paul knew how hard Gregg had been practicing his pitch. "There's a pitching game later. Want to do that with me, pal?"

"Cool!" Then he looked up at his mother. "That okay?"

She laughed, the most carefree sound Paul had ever heard from her. "Absolutely." She leaned forward, her voice a mock whisper. "I throw like a girl, you know."

Her unique green eyes were bright, her skin creamy ivory. And her mouth, curved in a natural smile, was winsome, beckoning. He hadn't needed reminding that she was a girl. She was all too feminine with her loose, dark hair, a gold locket twinkling at her throat. Instead of wearing a T-shirt, she had on a cotton blouse the same color as her eyes that emphasized her small waist.

Paul didn't realize he was staring until Gregg tugged repeatedly on his arm. "What?"

"The baby's got stuff dripping out of his mouth."

Paul jerked his attention back to Toby.

"He's cutting teeth," Laura explained, as she pulled a tissue from her tote bag. "Aren't you, big boy? I bet he'd like something cool on those gums." She looked up at Paul. "Should we find something?"

He was still off-kilter. "What?"

"For the baby…for his gums. Something cool," she repeated slowly, when it was clear her words weren't getting through.

"Sure. Right. I was going to ask Robin if she brought any teething biscuits."

"Not Jennifer?" Laura asked. "Maybe she has something cold for him in her diaper bag. I used to carry a gel-filled teething ring I'd frozen at home."

"Jen's not feeling too good. I thought I'd let her have some time with Alec…without bothering her."

Laura's gaze followed his to the shady spot beneath the oak where the pair sat. "It's not anything serious, is it?" She shook her head. "Silly thing to say. If it were, she wouldn't be here. But you're right. I'm sure we can find something for this little guy without bothering Jennifer." She looked around the growing crowd. "Is Robin here?"

"I haven't seen them yet." But he hadn't been paying attention to the other people in the church-yard, either. It was still difficult to pull his attention from Laura.

"I imagine there are ice cubes in the kitchen re-frigerator. I can wrap a small towel around one, let him suck on it." She leaned closer to Toby. "How does that sound?"

The baby gurgled, responding to her voice.

"It'll only take me a minute."

Gregg tugged at her arm. "Mom, can I go play with Philip and Bobby?"

She looked where a few other boys around Gregg's age had congregated. "Fine. But don't leave the yard. For anything," she emphasized.

He took off on a run. She stared after him.

"He'll be okay." Paul jiggled Toby. "I have to watch out for Lexi, so I'll make sure they both stay in sight."

"Doesn't seem like it was any time since he was Toby's age," she said wistfully.

He would have thought she'd be glad Gregg was getting older, less dependent on her. He watched as she hurried away to the Sunday school building. He took the time while she was gone to notice that Jer and Alec were still sitting quietly in the shade. Then Toby decided he wanted the buttons on Paul's shirt.

"There was plenty of ice." Laura was breathless as she arrived back. "And one of the ladies had a clean hankie." She had wrapped the ice cube so the baby wouldn't get an ice burn.

He offered it to Toby. "Here you go, tiger."

The baby clutched at the ice and then sucked on it greedily when Paul put it to his lips.

Laura stroked his fine, blond hair. "Poor little guy. Those gums must be hurting."

"Life's rough at his age." Paul tucked him closer to his body and Toby settled.

"Maybe he's already thinking about what he'll be when he grows up," Laura countered with a definite twinkle in her eyes.

Paul chuckled. "Jen says he's going to be the family veterinarian. He pulls their dog's ears, then kisses him better."

"I was sure Kirsten was going to be a ballerina. But after years of classes, she decided that tutus were dumb, and that ended that." She adjusted the handkerchief that Toby was tugging on.

"She's smart." He looked over to make sure Gregg and Lexi were still in sight. "She'll make something of herself."

"Just as long as she's happy." There was such longing in her words that it took him aback.

"Any reason to think she won't be?"

"Oh, no!" Her hands fluttered. "Of course not. I didn't mean…"

She wasn't thinking only of Kirsten. She was thinking of herself. The realization hit with a certainty he didn't question. "Everyone wants their kids to have things better than they did."

Her eyes, in a rare unguarded moment, met his. In them he read vulnerability and sadness. And also hope. "I want her to be…free. Not tethered to anything in the past…"

He hesitated. "But we all have a past. It's part of who we are."

Shadows darkened her eyes. "You think so?"

"I wouldn't be who I am if I hadn't grown up worrying about my kid brothers and sisters. It's not a bad thing, just part of me."

"Hey, you two, it's a picnic, not a wake!" His brother, Ben, grinned, slapping Paul on the back. The guy could coax a smile out of a mannequin.

"Well, we are at the church." Paul's voice was droll. "And there's a *ton* of food. Could be confusing…."

"Oh, you!" Robin giggled. "Hi, Laura! Isn't it a great day for the picnic? I was afraid it might rain, but Ben *never* thinks it's going to rain." She wriggled her toddler's hand in her own. "And I didn't want to disappoint this one."

"So we're all on toddler duty," Paul replied.

"Not to make too fine a point of it, but doesn't Toby have parents of his own?" Ben asked, making a face for his nephew's benefit.

"Jen's not well." Paul nodded toward her.

Ben frowned. "Then why's she here?"

"She says she's just tired."

Ben put an arm around his wife. "Maybe she is. That happens with expectant mothers."

"Maybe," Paul said.

"Don't fret so much," Robin chided. "You've been watching over the family long enough. If Alec's looking out for her, Jen'll be fine."

Shifting Toby so that the boy could see his parents, he noticed Laura staring at him oddly. "Gregg okay?"

She pointed to a patch of grass not swarming with picnickers. "He and the other boys are kicking a soccer ball."

He set the toddler on his feet and the boy lurched forward. "I think Toby's getting restless."

"I'd better check on the kids." Laura said.

It was an excuse. He could see it in her face. But he didn't have a reason to keep her there. Not one he wanted to examine.

"Laura!" Annie called to her as she jogged closer. "I'm glad you're here. Can you believe all the food? We have enough to feed the town! The other girls are here, too. Of course, Katherine is, but days like this she's pretty much on duty."

"I was afraid I might not see you in this crowd," Laura said.

Annie pushed her sunglasses up to rest on her head. "Not to worry. I can always find my friends. Why don't we go check out the dessert table?"

Laughing, Laura fell in step beside her. "Dessert first?"

"Always."

They strolled past the table filled with every cake, pie and cobbler imaginable.

Annie sniffed. "I think I'm already on a sugar high."

Leah, dressed to the nines, as usual, waved as she put a plate of animal-shaped cookies on the table. The thick frosting was realistically shaped into great whisker swirls and winking eyes.

"Those are incredible," Laura said.

"My son loves them. And now it's my signature dish." Leah dusted her hands, dislodging bits of powdered sugar. "So, is Annie taking you on a dessert prowl?"

"Guilty," Annie confessed, not looking a bit repentant. "Have you seen Grace or Emma?"

"They're setting up games. Cindy's in charge of recreation this year and she's put them to work. I barely escaped. So, have you guys picked out a spot?"

Annie propped her hands on her hips. "Somewhere shady. My skin will fry otherwise."

Laura glanced at the copse of oak trees on the north end of the lawn, where Jennifer was.

Leah looked in the same direction. "That would be perfect."

"I'll grab my quilt," Annie said. "And let Grace and Emma know where we're sitting."

As Laura approached the trees, she took the quilt from her tote bag. Shaking it out, she spread it on the grass. It didn't take the others long to join her.

Elizabeth and Charles waved to her as they escorted their parents to seats. Soon their children and grandchildren piled up, filling the long table. Eventually Jennifer got up to sit with her family.

Laura paused to say hello before she collected Gregg and Kirsten. They'd spend most of the afternoon with their friends once the games started, but she wanted them to have lunch together. And it was festive with the other families sitting quilt to quilt with them.

However, not long after they had eaten, the kids grew restless. She and Gregg agreed to meet for the three-legged race and then the kids took off. She didn't mind. Her friends' children disappeared, too, leaving the adults to talk. Ethan sprawled out for a nap and the other husbands wandered away.

Annie munched on a brownie. "I already had a piece of pie. I'm hopeless."

Leah batted away a fly. "If that's your worst flaw…" She broke off a bite of her cupcake, then looked at Laura. "How're things going at work these days?"

"About the same, I guess."

"And Paul?" Leah asked, then popped the bite of cupcake into her mouth.

"He's…okay."

Annie brushed crumbs from her jeans. "I don't think she's inquiring after his health."

"What?"

Leah rolled her eyes. "He was staring a hole through you this morning. You didn't notice?"

Fidgeting, Laura tried to remember if anything different had passed between them. "I was just helping him entertain his nephew."

"Uh-huh." Leah peeled the wrapper from the bottom of the cupcake. "It's okay if you don't want to tell us."

"There's nothing to tell," Laura protested weakly. Annie didn't seem convinced. "Really."

"I suppose we ought to go see if we can help with the games." Mercifully, Annie changed the subject.

Relieved, Laura agreed. Funny that Leah would think she'd seen something different about Paul.

But she didn't have time to dwell on it once she got caught up with the balloon toss. Avoiding being splashed with one of the water-filled balloons kept her busy. The time sped by and suddenly it was the three-legged race.

She met Gregg in the field behind the church and they got their sack. As they were each fitting a leg inside, Paul and Lexi took the spot next to them.

"Hey, guys!" Gregg was all smiles.

Little Lexi grinned shyly.

"I have to warn you. Lexi's fast as the wind." Paul pulled the sack up over his leg. "Of course she's got to drag me along with her."

Lexi giggled.

Gregg tugged on Laura's hand and she bent down to hear him whisper, "It's okay, Mom. We can go faster."

For his sake, she hoped they didn't come in last. When everyone was ready, stretched out in a line across the lawn, Cindy blew the whistle. Laura and Gregg got off to a quick start. Like a bunch of bobbing bowling pins, the group staggered forward. She clutched the edge of the sack, trying to keep her balance as they jigged toward the halfway mark. Gregg set up a steady rhythm and she was amazed that they were one of the leading teams.

She darted a glance to her side and saw that Paul and his niece were neck and neck with them. She clumped forward. Gregg wore a look of fierce determination. And to her relief, the finish line was close. In sync, she and Gregg went a little faster. They were only about six feet from the end. Still in tandem, they closed the distance.

Then Laura's foot got caught in a depression in the grass. They spilled face-first to the ground. Laura held out her arms to break the fall, but she still clipped her chin. Tangled with her son who had fallen on top of her, she struggled to get up, to get back in the race, but flopped instead to one side as the sack twisted around their legs.

"Give me your other hand," Paul said as he pulled her to a sitting position.

Gregg scrambled out of the sack, staring at the other competitors as they cheered from the other side of the finish line.

Paul peeled the sack off Laura's legs, then helped her stand. "You all right?"

"Oh, sure." She ignored the throbbing of her knees and one hand.

He tipped up her chin. "Should put some ice on that."

"You didn't have to stop for us." She trembled beneath his touch.

"Lexi's a good sport. She didn't mind." He brushed off some dried grass that clung to her arm.

Laura tried to check Gregg for injuries but he squirmed under her inspection. "I'm okay, Mom."

"I'm sorry, bud." She straightened his ball cap. "I didn't see that hole."

"Me, neither." Gregg had already recovered from the loss. "Can I go do the apple bob thing with the guys now?"

"Sure." She dusted off her pants as he loped toward his friends.

Lexi still clung to her uncle's hand, though, The difference in girls and boys. The dark-eyed, dark-haired child looked like a little princess.

Laura remembered the days when she could dress Kirsten like a doll. "You sure look pretty today, Lexi."

She stuck out one of her pink tennis shoes. "Mommy let me wear my new shoes."

"She did? Wow. What a nice mommy you have."

Paul looked over his shoulder, back at the crowd. "Why don't we go check in with Mommy?"

Laura suddenly felt like a fifth wheel. "I'll see you then."

"Do you want to say hi to Jen?" Paul's suggestion took her aback.

"Yeah, I would."

As they started walking in the direction of the picnic table where all the Russells had congregated, they could see it was deserted.

Paul felt a sickening thud in his gut. Something was wrong. He picked up the pace, searching the crowd, not seeing any of his family. As they reached the parking lot, they ran into Ben.

Paul could tell from his brother's face that his instinct was right. Ben glanced down at Lexi, then mouthed *hospital*. "Everyone's already gone. I waited for you."

What if Jen was losing the baby this time?

Paul felt Laura touch his arm. "Would it be all right if I take care of Lexi while you and Ben check on things?"

He wasn't sure. Lexi didn't need to be scared about her mother, but…

"You have my cell number," Laura continued.

"And I can meet up with you in five minutes if necessary."

"She's right," Ben agreed.

Paul knelt to face his niece. "Ben and I have to take care of some things. Will you mind Laura while I'm gone?"

"Uh-huh. Can I have another cookie?"

"Sure, baby." He stood. "I'll call as soon as I know something." He glanced backward as they rushed to Ben's car. Laura waved as they drove past.

He imagined all the possibilities as Ben sped through the quiet streets, reaching the hospital in record time. Their family filled the waiting room, some sitting in the chairs and couches, others pacing.

Ben had given him the barest details. Jen had fainted and her pulse was erratic. It could be as simple as the heat or fatigue…or it could be a lot worse.

Alec's face was pale and he clutched Toby.

"Do they know anything yet?" Paul asked, seeing the agony on his brother-in-law's face.

"They're doing tests. I just couldn't believe it when she toppled over like that. She was only a few feet away from me. Then she collapsed…." He clutched his son even closer. "And I hadn't done anything to stop it."

"Doesn't sound like you could have." Paul clapped him on the back. "It must have happened so fast she would have fallen even if you had been right next to her."

"And pregnant women faint all the time," Ben reassured him.

But they all knew this had been a difficult pregnancy.

Unable to sit, Paul joined the others who paced the room. Time moved with excruciating deliberation. Every time they heard the squeak of rubber-soled shoes pausing near the doorway, everyone looked up.

The cell phone in his pocket vibrated, but Paul ignored it. Nothing was more important than knowing if Jennifer would be all right. It had been hours. Shouldn't they know something by now?

A shadow fell across the doorway and Paul stood at attention. But it wasn't a doctor or nurse. Laura, holding Lexi's hand, entered the waiting room. Lexi ran to Elizabeth. "Grammy, where's Mommy?"

Laura looked at him helplessly, then beckoned him to come closer. "I'm sorry, but after a while, she was getting scared. You were all gone and she doesn't really know me. I tried to call, but you didn't answer."

He drove his fingers through his hair. "I'm sorry. I blanked out Lexi. We still haven't heard anything."

She touched his arm, a tentative, gentle gesture. "That's not necessarily bad. Tests take such a long time, and I'm sure they want to be thorough."

She was right, but it didn't make waiting any easier. "I'm sorry you had to come here. I should have—"

"I wanted to. Kirsten's spending the night with Mandy, and Gregg's at his grandparents. I'd like to stay…if that's all right." Her eyes met his, and he read her concern.

He turned to look at Lexi, who was cuddled in Elizabeth's arms and seemed to be okay. "I can't believe I forgot all about her. I told Mother she was with you when I first got here, then…"

"Then you were worried about your sister. Please don't apologize. Lexi and I had fun at first." She touched a hand-painted butterfly on her cheek. "Face painting kept us busy for a while. Lexi insisted that I would look good in glitter." She turned so that the light picked up the sparkling edges of the design.

"I didn't think it would take this long. Guess I was hoping they'd say Jen's fine, go on home."

She leaned forward. "Maybe they still will. From my experience, hospitals seem to go into slow mode on weekends. So everything takes longer."

"They had to locate her OB. But he got here pretty fast once they did." It occurred to him that she had probably become familiar with hospitals when Jerry got sick. For his part, hospitals still made him uncomfortable. All those surgeries his father had endured…The bleak veterans' hospital, the colorless walls, the pain in his father's face.

"Would you like some coffee?" she was asking.

"I don't want to leave—"

"I'll go." She checked with the others and Robin and Sharon accompanied her to the cafeteria.

The women came back with trays of coffee along with drinks for the children. Laura had put the correct amount of sugar in his. He took a few swallows.

As it got later, Robin decided to take her children home. She collected Toby, as well. But Lexi cried to stay with her father. Elizabeth coaxed the child into stretching out on the couch as she cradled her head. Soon she was asleep.

Charles flexed his legs and Paul knew his father was stiffening up. "You two could head home. I'll stay here."

"It's all right, son." Charles shifted in the chair. "I can't rest until I know Jen's fine."

Since he couldn't, either, Paul understood. Laura came back in, carrying more coffee. He hadn't noticed her leaving. She'd brought hot chocolate for his father, Charles's favorite. And she had fetched the quilt from her car, which she and Elizabeth spread over Lexi.

Thoughtful, quiet gestures. She looked up just then with a reassuring smile. *I think you ought to know the real Laura. The one underneath all that emotional abuse. You may think she's weak, but it takes a strong woman to protect her children, to take on the challenges she has.*

The real Laura...Then who had the real Jerry been?

* * *

By midnight, Paul found himself staring out the windows to the nearly empty parking lot.

"Hospitals are always off-putting at night." Laura held her hand up to the window, blocking some of the light from the lamppost.

"Did you stay the nights with Jerry…when he was hospitalized?"

She crossed her arms. "A lot of them. I alternated with his mother. She wanted to stay all the time, but she's older, not really able to. I thought it would be a terrible thing if Jerry woke up and found himself all alone. Because he knew…that it was terminal. It's not a time to be alone."

He examined her face, still unable to determine what sort of relationship she'd had with Jerry. "Would he have done the same for you?"

Pain zigzagged through her expression, then disappeared. "Probably not. But that's not why I did it."

"Why then?" he persisted.

"He was my children's father. And, once, a long time ago, he was the man of my dreams."

He shifted to face her. "You loved him?"

Sorrow darkened her eyes. "I used to."

"What happened, Laura?"

She closed her eyes briefly. "Our marriage happened. And it wasn't good. Or fine. Or anything

I'd hoped it would be. And after a while I stopped hoping."

The squeak of rubber-soled shoes intruded on the quiet. He wanted to ask more, know more, but the doctor was talking to Alec.

"She's stable." Doctor Farley looked as tired as most of them felt. "I want her to stay with us for the time being, then bed rest at home."

"How's the baby?" Alec asked, not hiding his fear.

"Strong as a horse." The doctor tugged on his stethoscope. "It's Jennifer I'm worried about. She's toxic and some of the edema's in her lungs."

Alec steadied his voice. "Can I see her?"

"Briefly. She's resting. I want her to stay quiet, so no other visitors tonight."

Alec followed the doctor from the waiting room. Paul and the rest of the family members looked at each other, then Charles stood, his gait slow, and they all gathered in a circle. He led them in a prayer, thanking the Lord for Jennifer's recovery and beseeching Him to continue watching over her. After exchanging hugs, they started filtering out, heading home. Lexi remained asleep on the couch.

"I'll just be a minute," Paul said. "I want to walk Laura to her car."

"That's all right. I can—"

"I'll walk you out." It might be Rosewood, but it

was well past midnight and the parking lot was practically deserted.

She was quiet as they passed through the hushed corridors of the hospital and out to her car. Her alarm chirped as she clicked the remote.

He opened her door and waited until she'd slid inside to close it.

She lowered the window. "I'm glad Jennifer's going to be okay. I...your father's prayer really touched me."

It had touched him, too. "We prayed for Jen when we first got to the hospital, but Dad taught us it's as important to thank the Lord as it is to ask Him for help."

Laura put her key in the ignition. "I'll remember that."

"Thanks, Laura." He rubbed the door handle absently. "It meant a lot to me that you stayed tonight."

Her lips curved into a smile. "Good night then."

"Night." He stepped away as she started the car, then pulled out of the parking space. With the dim lamplight to guide him, he walked slowly back to the entrance. And wondered again at the woman who had somehow come to mean so much to him.

Chapter Fifteen

❧

Laura slipped the card from Elizabeth Russell back into the envelope. The note thanked Laura for her help the past few weeks since Jennifer had been in the hospital. All she had done was bring over casseroles a few times, since she had known that Elizabeth was spending most of her time at the hospital. And now Jennifer was home, Alec hovering over her. The best part—her prognosis was excellent.

Checking the clock, she frowned. Kirsten should have been home an hour ago. She had homework and needed to study for a big history test. She heard the front door open. That was probably her, since Paul had taken Gregg to practice at the batting cages.

Kirsten strolled into the kitchen.

Laura laid the envelope on the counter. "You're an hour late."

Her daughter shrugged.

"Did you hear me?"

"I'm two feet away from you. Of course I heard."

Gritting her teeth, Laura counted to three. "So, why are you late?"

Kirsten opened the refrigerator and studied the contents. Her voice was muffled when she replied, "I dunno."

"Kirsten, that's the third time this week," Laura admonished, rubbing the crease in her forehead, willing away the nagging headache. "I've tried to be understanding since your grandparents moved here, but you can't ignore my rules."

"But you're just making the rules to keep me away from them."

Patience didn't seem to be the answer. "If you don't listen, I'll be forced to ground you."

Kirsten slammed the refrigerator door. "But the big party is this week!"

"I want you to be able to see your friends, but you have to do as I say."

"Nana says we might be moving back to Houston."

Laura forced herself to remain calm. "That's wishful thinking on her part. My job is here. Our new lives are here."

For a moment, Kirsten looked uncertain. "Then why are you trying to keep us from seeing Nana and Grandpa?"

"I'm not, sweetie." Not for the first time she

wished her in-laws hadn't moved to Rosewood. "I know how much they mean to you...how much they love you. I want you to spend time with them, but I don't want you to ignore what I say." The doorbell rang. "What now?"

A man she didn't recognize stood on the front porch. "Laura Manning?"

She didn't know why, but she suddenly had the worst premonition. "Yes."

"Sign here." He handed her a clipboard and pen.

Her hand shook as she signed her name.

He handed her a trifolded sheaf of papers. The first word in bold letters seemed to swim before her eyes. *Subpoena.*

"Mom, what is it?"

"I don't know...yet."

Legs wobbly, Laura headed into the living room and sank into a chair. Slowly she unfolded the papers. It took her a while to absorb it all. Her in-laws were suing for custody.

"Mom?"

Laura lifted her head. "Sweetie, would you mind if I have a little time alone?"

"Are you okay?"

Sickened yet strangely numb, Laura gripped the papers. "I'm not sure."

"Do you want me to call Nana and Grandpa?"

Laura's stomach knotted. "Thanks, sweetie, but

no. I...don't really want to see them right now."
She considered that she should be attending to
Kirsten. But she was too shattered. Meredith had
money and clout on her side. What if she won? How
would she live without her children? All of Jerry's
accusations that she wasn't a good mother resurfaced. He had always said she didn't have the education, the background, the breeding to raise the
children properly.

It was getting dark inside the house, but Laura
didn't turn on the light. The darkness had already
seeped into her heart. Remotely she heard a car
stop, the murmur of voices interspersed with
laughter. Then the front door was pushed open. Paul
had brought Gregg home from practice.

"Why're you sitting in the dark?" Gregg asked,
bounding into the room.

She reached for him, engulfing him in a greedy
hug. He complied, then wriggled back.

"Everything okay?" Paul asked.

She felt tears bubbling near the surface. "Gregg,
I think Kirsten's waiting for you upstairs to help
with your homework."

"Okay. Can I have a soda?"

"Sure, sweetie. Take one up for Kirsten, too."

He scampered into the kitchen and Paul clicked
on a lamp. "What's up?"

Wordlessly, she handed him the subpoena.

He scanned the paper, his face grim. "What is she thinking?"

Laura shook her head. "I know we're not close, but I never thought…"

"Edward probably went along because he's been used to giving Meredith her way," Paul muttered.

Laura bent her head, hot tears escaping. "Oh, Paul, what am I going to do?"

He knelt beside her, grasping her arms. "You're going to fight. And you're going to win."

"I feel so outnumbered."

"You and the kids, you belong together."

"You'll be on our side?" she asked cautiously.

He rubbed her cold arms. "Did you think I wouldn't?"

"With Jerry…and it's his parents…"

"I don't know exactly what was between you and Jerry, but I do know that you and your children belong together. And, if Jerry were alive, he would agree."

"You…you believe that?"

Paul tightened his hands around her arms. "No matter what you're thinking, don't even consider giving up."

Her lips trembled. "My babies," she whispered.

He pulled her close and her tears soaked his shirt. "I know," he said.

It had been so long since she'd been held—protected. Unaccustomed to depending on anyone else, she tried to tell herself that she had to stay strong, she shouldn't lean. That he would try to control her, too. But she was tired. And, maybe, just maybe she'd been wrong about him.

Laura thought the worst part would be telling the children. Gregg was puzzled, but immediately voiced his desire to stay with her. Kirsten was quiet, watchful. And though it pained her to admit it, Laura wasn't sure what her daughter's choice would be.

But the outpouring of support in the following weeks was beyond her. Annie and Ethan, the other women she had met through church, and most especially Paul's family, overwhelmed her. Each offered to testify on her behalf. Donna insisted she was available day or night at a moment's notice. And Paul arranged to pay for all the legal fees.

And he came to see them every day. His bond with Gregg grew so strong that Laura couldn't imagine her son's disappointment if Paul were no longer in his life. She didn't dwell on her own. And, although Kirsten was more reluctant, she was also drawn in by Paul.

As she and the kids drove to the Russell's home, Laura tried not to think about the approaching court date. Deciding to trust in the words of the scripture, she continued to allow the children to visit their grandparents. She was still afraid, but she refused to let the fear dictate their lives.

Once inside, Laura tried to relax. At least as much as was possible these days. Familiar with Paul's siblings, she listened as they squabbled good-naturedly in the kitchen. Then she wandered into the conservatory where she could watch the kids out back through the windows. Since the arrival of the summons, she felt as if they might be snatched away at any time. She knew it wasn't rational, but she couldn't help it.

The hardwood floor creaked behind her, and she turned.

Elizabeth looked startled. "I didn't know anyone was in here."

"Just needed a moment," Laura explained.

"I imagine you need time alone quite often these days." Elizabeth gestured to the chairs. "Can I join you?"

"Of course."

Elizabeth sank into one of the armchairs. "You know, Paul's sometimes a quiet man, a thinker. Not that he's not a doer, too, but he has to consider all the angles and consequences of a situation. It's come in handy with his work. He could have made some frightful mistakes otherwise. But one thing you never have to doubt is his loyalty."

"Why are you telling me this?"

"Paul's been fiercely loyal to Jerry and it's hard for him to let that go." Elizabeth fiddled with the long chain at her neck. "I hope you don't mind, but we've talked and he said he doesn't know any of the details of your problems with Jerry."

"It's been…hard." Laura hooked one foot under her leg as she sat.

Elizabeth patted her hand. "Of course it has. I know what you're thinking—how can you tell unpleasant truths about a dead man? But you're not giving my son the credit he deserves. He might not like everything he hears, but don't assume that he won't believe you."

Laura picked at the pillow wedged beside her. "You're more certain than I am."

Elizabeth patted her arm. "Don't you think it's time Paul knew everything?"

Laura bit her lip. "What if he doesn't stand beside me…once he knows?"

"Like I said, I don't think you're crediting Paul with the understanding I happen to know he has. You haven't had a very fair shake in the past, but I think you'll see that's changed."

"I told Paul how lucky he is to have you for a mother."

Elizabeth gave her a small hug. "Now I'm going to give you what you wanted—some time alone."

"It's funny, but that's not what I want anymore. I don't suppose you could just sit here for a bit?"

"You read my mind. That's exactly what I want."

In the hall, Paul backed away. He knew his mother well enough to see that she had given Laura her seal of approval. Even though she was a likable, generally easygoing woman, Elizabeth was fiercely protective of her children. And that approval didn't come without a lot of consideration. But she'd liked Laura from the start. He'd always valued his mother's wisdom and this was no exception.

She'd gotten it right.

Chapter Sixteen

Paul pulled the Rover over to the side of the road. It was a quiet spot, one only a few cars passed. He and Laura had been scouting properties. But he couldn't concentrate on anything he'd seen.

She stared out at the fields of waving grass. "Is there supposed to be a house here?"

"No. How about stretching our legs?"

"Okay." She opened the car door and strolled to the edge of the field, shading her eyes. "Late-blooming bluebonnets."

But he didn't look at the flowers. "You know, it's not easy getting you alone. At the office, people can walk in any time, and the kids are at your house."

She knelt to pick a blade of grass. "Any special reason you want to be alone?"

"I want to talk."

She looked suddenly nervous. "Should I be worried?"

"Just the opposite."

Her eyes widened.

He didn't prolong the suspense. "I haven't wanted to believe I could be wrong about Jerry."

"And now?"

"Can you tell me about it?"

"It didn't happen all at once." She clasped her hands together. "And, at first, I was happy with him. I was young and I knew I had a lot to learn, but nothing was ever quite good enough—from the way I combed my hair, to the clothes I chose, to the way I kept house." She walked toward a mature maple tree surrounded by saplings. "So I tried harder. I just wanted to please Jerry, for us to have the kind of marriage my parents didn't. But I hadn't gotten to know him very well before we married."

He followed her. "What was the rush?"

"My life at home was pretty awful. I told you how much I loved my grandmother, but she had been gone for a while. My parents fought nonstop. Neither of them cared about me." She ran her fingers over a tender branch of one of the saplings. "During one of their fights I learned I'd been a mistake they blamed on each other. I just tried to stay out of their way, but the fights went on day and night. The nights were the worst—the screaming and threats that kept me awake."

It sounded awful.

Her voice was strained. "I suppose I would have done anything to get out of there, but I really did love Jerry. You know how he was—so charming and popular. I thought I was the luckiest girl on the planet…."

"And?" *What had changed?*

"Then the criticism began, but I thought that was normal since I didn't have any role models. And Kirsten came along. The criticism got worse and I wanted to believe it was because he was worried about his daughter." She released the branch. "I didn't have many people to discuss it with. He didn't want me to have any friends. The only one I kept was Donna. We'd known each other since grade school and she knew how bad my home life was and didn't judge. Still, I felt pretty isolated." She took a few steps, pausing at the massive trunk of the parent tree. "He told me I was being selfish—that I had everything any woman could want and that I should be grateful. So I tried harder. That's when Jerry seemed to get meaner. He went from criticizing to being verbally abusive, always berating, belittling, telling me how ignorant I was."

He resisted the urge to take her arms. "Did it get physical?"

"I would have left him because I know that can

extend to the children. But, between the steady criticism and name-calling, every bit of confidence I had disappeared. He constantly told me how ignorant and inept I was—that my lack of breeding was apparent in all my mistakes—and that I was just like my parents." She leaned back against the tree, as though she needed the support. "He said I'd failed by having a girl instead of a boy. That I'd been a failure and disappointment from the beginning. And since he never talked that way when other people were around, I began to think he was right. It sounds stupid, I know. But my family was my whole life. Jerry wouldn't let me have a job or go to college after we got married. Then, of course, I had Kirsten to care for. And all I'd ever wanted was a happy family."

Sickened, Paul felt like slamming his fist into the tree. Instead he reached for Laura's hand. He had acknowledged to himself that he had been wrong about Jerry, but this...

"Jerry controlled everything. Money, where we lived, our social lives, who I could see. If I tried to protest, he got ugly, but never when the kids could see. And I didn't want them to see. I'd lived with that when I was a kid and it was awful. So I gave in rather than fight."

He rubbed her knuckles with his thumb. "Did that help?"

"You'd think it would." She tightened her grasp

on his hand. "Instead, thinking back, I believe it egged him on."

Paul had witnessed this kind of behavior before. The strong picking on the weak simply because they could. Like a bully taking away a kid's lunch money, the abuse generally got worse when the victim bowed to the pressure.

"I was even dumb enough to believe that when we had Gregg, Jerry might change. Now he had his boy. But he ignored him. Pretty much like he'd done with Kirsten."

Paul couldn't understand any man doing that. "They talk like they really loved him."

"Children who are ignored try even harder," she replied quietly. "Kirsten adored her father even though he was aloof. And that made me try harder. I didn't want them to be unhappy."

"Did you ever think about leaving?"

"Often. But Jerry said that if I did, he'd make sure I never saw the kids again." She lifted her chin. "And that was worse than anything else he could have said."

The bright sun overhead seemed to mock them. Paul couldn't imagine living with that fear, or with someone who wanted to destroy you.

Laura shifted the telephone so that it rested on her shoulder. "Sometimes, I think the custody battle is a sort of surreal nightmare."

Donna clucked in sympathy. "How are you coping...day to day?"

"I go to work, take care of the kids in the evening and pray that everything will turn out all right." She put her feet on the ottoman, staring out the living room window. The kids were with their friends and the house was uncommonly still. As it would be if she lost them.

"You know I can be there in a matter of hours."

Laura's throat tightened. "I know. And I may take you up on that." She paused. "I told Paul today."

Donna didn't have to ask what. "How'd he take it?"

"I...I think he understood."

"It's better that he knows."

Laura knew that. Still, it was a huge thing. "He considered Jerry a brother. I think it hurts him to realize he had another side."

Donna sighed. "It hurt a lot of people. But you can get beyond him, Laura."

She stared out at her elderly neighbors, walking hand in hand down the sidewalk. "I suppose."

"Do you need money? I have some saved...."

"Thank you, but no." Laura hesitated. "I may not have said it lately, but your friendship is a blessing."

"That works both ways. Will you call if you need me? Just to talk even?"

Laura brushed a tear from her cheek. "You can count on it."

* * *

When Paul didn't get an answer at the front door, he walked around the house. The creaking of the gate gave him away and Laura turned.

"I did try ringing the bell," he explained.

"The kids are at their grandparents."

"Ah." No wonder she looked so down.

She picked a yellowing leaf from the rosebush. "I'm trying really hard not to be bothered by it. I know they need their grandparents…."

Paul took her by the arm. "Why don't we sit in the swing?"

After they sat side by side, she looked up at him. "And this helps, how?"

He set the swing gently in motion. "Nothing ever seems as bad when you're in a swing."

Between the columbine and roses in her garden, a patch of Grecian windflowers flourished. They reminded him of her, their stems often bent nearly to the ground in the wind, looking so fragile, but in reality strong, springing back to an upright position once the wind died.

Twilight settled and they listened to the chirping of cicadas. It was Paul's favorite time of the day, that nether land between day and night. Other than the occasional barking of a nearby dog, little else was stirring.

"You're right," she said finally. "This is helping."

She was soft beside him and felt, well...right. "Do you remember how I was when you first moved here?"

She chuckled and he liked the way her gentle laugh resonated. "Oh, yes."

"I was wrong."

Her eyes met his and he heard the catch of her breath. "You were?"

"Yeah."

He could see the quickening of her pulse in her throat and her lips parted. "Oh?"

"It's not easy for me to admit a mistake." He eased her hair back from her face. "But I'm glad you decided to come to Rosewood."

Chapter Seventeen

Laura looked out her kitchen window as she rinsed glasses. She was learning to accept help. When Kirsten continued acting out, disobeying Laura, Paul had stepped in. And her daughter responded to him. Laura realized she had been able to depend on him more in the short time she had known him than on Jerry in all of their marriage.

Depositions had begun. One by one, Laura's friends had been deposed. And even though each reported that it had gone well, Laura worried. She still didn't know what Kirsten would tell the judge once the trial began. Meredith not only promised a return to her large home, but also a huge allowance, clothing and pretty much anything else the teenager wanted. It might mean losing, but Laura couldn't bring herself to compete. No limitations wasn't the way to raise a child.

Gregg remained a constant. His already solid relationship with Paul had grown stronger. Having always craved more of his father's attention, he was happy with Paul's. And he had made it clear he didn't want to leave his mother, despite anything his grandparents promised.

Although Laura turned more and more to prayer, she couldn't help questioning why the Lord was putting her through this. If she couldn't have had a loving husband or parents, why couldn't she at least be sure of keeping her children?

Elizabeth was a great source of strength, telling her to trust in the Lord, that He wouldn't fail her. But Laura wasn't sure her newly burgeoning faith could stand the test.

So Paul was coming over to pray with her. It took a strong man to live his faith, to follow it in today's world. And she was coming to learn just how strong Paul was.

Kirsten and Gregg liked going to church, but they had never experienced a family devotional. Laura briefed them. It troubled her when Kirsten fell silent.

Gregg heard Paul at the door before she did and opened it. Laura had prepared a simple dinner, which she served outside. No phone or television.

Kirsten only picked at her food.

"How was school?" Paul asked her.

"Okay."

"I hear the youth group's going on a trip to the Riverwalk." The popular San Antonio destination was one the kids really enjoyed.

"I guess so."

Paul met Laura's eyes, but she didn't know, beyond the purpose of the evening, what was bothering her daughter. Gregg took up the slack, chattering as the meal progressed.

Laura expected Kirsten to beg off once they began the devotional. Instead she watched and listened attentively. Paul chose a passage from Peter about strength.

When he was about to begin his prayer, Kirsten spoke up. "Could we pray for Mandy?"

"Sure." Again Paul looked at Laura in question.

"Is something wrong with her, sweetie?"

Kirsten's face crumpled. "She's got leukemia."

Shocked, Laura rose and embraced her daughter. "I'm so sorry, honey. When did you find out?"

"Today. Her parents talked to the doctor. She's been getting sick a lot, but they thought it was the flu." Her voice warbled. "Only it wasn't."

"They can do a lot for leukemia." Laura soothed her child, feeling immediate empathy for Mandy's parents. "I'm sure they're taking her to good doctors."

"And you can trust in the Lord," Paul reminded her quietly.

Gregg took his sister's hand. "We'll pray her better."

At his unquestioning trust, Laura didn't know what to say.

Fortunately Paul did. He took one hand of each child and they, in turn, clasped Laura's. His prayer was straightforward, sincere. As they prayed for Mandy's recovery, Laura felt the faith she had sought.

Kirsten squeezed her hand, hard. Laura wished she could protect her from hurt, the pain life could bring. Failing that, there was something she could do. Keep the Lord in their home.

The lavender fields between Fredericksburg and Stonewall were in full bloom. The acres of fragrant flowers swayed in the afternoon breeze.

It had been Paul's idea to bring Kirsten here. She desperately wanted to do something to help her friend, and Paul mentioned that his mother made pillows with lavender sewn inside to help his father sleep when his pain worsened.

The lavender estate sold all sorts of products—candles, bath oils, potpourri, gels, even bookmarks pressed with the delicate flowers. And, for their purpose, fresh-cut lavender.

Known for its soothing properties, the flower also helped combat stress. The fragrance was heady. Hoed rows of vibrant lavender contrasted with the red, sandy loam soil. Despite the Texas sun overhead, it felt as though they'd stepped into Provence.

"This was a wonderful idea," Laura murmured to Paul as she watched Kirsten wander through the gift shop.

"I know what it is to want to do something, anything, to help."

"Your mother said you helped hold the family together through your dad's ordeal."

He put a candle back on the shelf. "She's exaggerating."

"It's what you do, isn't it?"

Paul looked at her, his expression unguarded. "Family means everything to me."

He was the sort of man who would treasure his own wife and children.

"Mom?" Kirsten held up a small tube. "Could we get Mandy this gel, too?"

"Sure." She opened her hand to show Kirsten the bookmarks she'd picked up. "I thought you and Mandy could each have one." The mementos were tied with hand-dyed silk ribbon.

"Thanks, Mom."

Laura opened her other hand. "And these are charms for your bracelets." Each one was clear with a tiny, preserved flower inside. "They will remind you of each other when you wear them." She had also picked up bath salts, sachets and a wreath to place in a basket for Mandy's parents. "Would you go round up your brother? I think we're ready to check out."

Once they were outside, Paul suggested a stop at his mother's favorite fabric store to collect everything else they needed to make the pillow. Gregg started to get restless and Paul promised to get some ball practice in later to help him run off his energy.

Back at the house, Laura and Kirsten spread everything out on the dining room table. She'd let her daughter choose the fabric.

"I think we'll have enough to make her a few matching sachets," Laura mused. "She could put them in her drawers."

"Mom?"

Laura threaded a needle. "Yes, sweetie?"

"Thanks for doing this."

"Of course. She's your friend. And, I really, really believe she's going to be all right."

"Nana doesn't believe much in prayer, does she?"

Laura bit her lip. She didn't want to be untruthful, but she also didn't want to run down her mother-in-law. "Faith is a very personal issue. I lost touch with my own for a while. I'm just grateful I found it again."

"Mom…do you like Paul?"

Laura pricked her finger. "Sure. You like him, too, don't you?"

"I mean like a guy. Do you like him like that?"

Laura knew only the truth would do. "I suppose so, but you don't have anything to worry about.

We…we have a lot of…well, I guess you'd call it baggage between us. So we're just friends."

"You mean Daddy?"

Laura nodded. "Paul was his friend."

"So you can't love him?"

The sudden ache in her heart was suffocating. But Laura did her best not to let it show. "It's complicated."

"Do you want to love him?" Kirsten persisted.

Laura bent her head. "It doesn't matter what I want." She hadn't wanted to care for Paul any more than she had wanted to choose wrong the first time. She cleared her throat. "Now, what do you think about those sachets?"

"That'd be okay." But Kirsten's eyes were clouded, a sure sign she hadn't been distracted.

It wasn't surprising, Laura realized. She hadn't been able to distract herself, either.

Chapter Eighteen

Laura and Paul pulled into the driveway of her in-laws' rented house to collect Gregg. Kirsten was spending the night with Mandy. Her friend was an only child and her parents had urged Laura to let the girls finish out the weekend together.

Laura considered the wisdom of having Paul accompany her, but didn't think it could do any more damage. Meredith had made her mind up about their relationship anyway.

Fortunately, it was Edward who opened the door. "Come in, come in." Benign as usual, he had never displayed any antagonism. Laura had even glimpsed his regret since they'd filed the court documents. But she doubted he would ever cross his wife. Habit or cowardice, it didn't really matter. She had a hold over him that he couldn't or wouldn't break.

Gregg was in the living room with his grand-mother. When he spotted Laura and Paul, he jumped up and ran over to them. "Guess what? Nana bought me a huge new tank and fish!"

"Honey, you've already got an aquarium."

"It's for over here," he explained. "But it's still mine. And she bought me all the fish I wanted."

"Nana should have fun taking care of them for you."

Meredith waved toward a pair of chairs. "I told you Gregg could stay the night."

Laura hated the tension in the room. "I know, but we have church in the morning."

Meredith frowned.

"You're welcome to join us." They weren't empty words. Laura wished her mother-in-law could find what she had.

"I don't think so." As Meredith spoke, her eyes were on Paul.

"I know my parents would enjoy seeing you," Paul added.

Meredith's expression wavered. "Your mother shared some photos with me…. That was kind of her."

"Mom's singing a special song tomorrow," Gregg told them.

"Laura? Singing?" Meredith asked, peering at her daughter-in-law.

"It's not anything important." Laura wasn't yet comfortable being singled out for attention.

"It is, too," Gregg insisted. "'Cause she's the best one."

Embarrassed, Laura nudged her son. "I'd better get this one home. Thank you both for taking care of him."

Edward said, "Our pleasure—"

Gregg threw his arms up in a hug and Edward hugged him back.

"We're going fishing next Saturday," Paul told him. "Why don't you come with us? Nothing fancy, but Gregg here makes it fun."

Gregg giggled.

Edward scratched his head. "That sounds like fun. I'll have to get some equipment."

"I've got everything we need. With a big family you always have extra."

Meredith looked uncertain, a rarity for her.

Laura glanced down at her son. "Give Nana a hug."

He did, then grinned. "Thanks for all the cool fish."

"You're welcome. You know where they are."

Laura tried not to look hurried as they left. Paul squeezed her arm as they drove to her house.

Once inside, she gave Gregg his instructions. "Bath and then bed."

"Can I have some cereal?"

"Okay, honey. But pick one that doesn't have sugar."

He obliged, ate his cereal quickly, then headed upstairs.

Laura sighed as she tidied up.

"What are you thinking?"

She put down the towel. "How did everything get so mixed up? Maybe if I hadn't left Houston in the first place…"

"Sorry you came here?"

She stared into his eyes and read his concern. Despite everything, she couldn't regret moving to Rosewood…meeting him. "You may not believe this, but it's the best thing I ever did."

He smoothed the hair that fell across her forehead. "You are amazing."

She felt her cheeks heat. "Amazing?"

"Amazing."

After church the next day, Laura and the kids joined Paul's family for lunch. Her singing was the topic of the day.

"You have an incredible voice!" Sharon placed a bowl of shrimp salad on the long table. They were serving buffet style. "I knew you sang in the choir, but I had no idea."

Face flushed, Laura smiled. "I love music."

"You blew me away." Ben deposited his toddler on the grass, holding the boy's fingers as he took a few wobbly steps. "Robin and I have kept you in our prayers. Things are going to turn out all right." He knelt down, following his son.

"I have, too. Kept you in my prayers." Sharon put a serving spoon into the salad. "And I know Jen and Alec have, too. The judge will see what a super mom you are."

Kevin, the youngest Russell brother, chased Lexi, making her giggle. But he overheard his sister and stopped by the table, filching a potato chip. "She's right. We're behind you, Laura."

"Thank you…everyone." Laura put the cheese-cake Jennifer loved on the side of the table with the desserts. "It means a lot, having all of you."

Elizabeth arrived with a basket of rolls. "Even though I got overruled on eating in the dining room, I have to agree the weather's too good to resist an outside lunch."

After lunch, some of the adults sat in lawn chairs scattered around the yard, watching the kids play soccer. Others helped out with the game. The tiniest kids were toddling around with Paul off to one side where he had a big, light ball they could push.

"He's so natural with them," Laura murmured.

"He was as excited as we were when the first grand-child came along." Elizabeth took the empty chair beside Laura, pulling it back into a patch of shade. Her husband and the grandparents sat closer to the kids on the other side of the yard. "I've always known he'd be a great father. He's crazy about your children."

"Yes," Laura replied, embarrassed that her voice had cracked.

Elizabeth patted her arm. "It's hard not to worry, but you'll win—I can't believe there'll be any other verdict."

Laura bowed her head. "Meredith has always gotten her way. Always."

"I know you've been trying your best with her. The Lord sees that."

Laura wiped her eyes. "I do have faith...."

"I know you've been praying to keep your children...." Elizabeth paused. "I don't want to make the mistake of interfering, but I do have another prayer you might try."

Laura looked up at her.

"You could pray *for* Meredith, to soften her heart."

It hadn't occurred to her that Meredith needed her prayers. Of course. "Thank you...for everything, for including us, for being on my side from the beginning."

"I sensed a lot about you the day we met. Call it mother's intuition."

Whatever it was, Laura was grateful.

Jennifer, so pregnant she was due any day, eased into a nearby lawn chair. "Someone will have to haul me out of this when it's time to go." The doctor had modified her bed rest. She still had to take it easy and spend part of each day in bed, but she could have small outings.

"How's our baby?" Elizabeth asked.

"Busy." Jennifer laid her hands on her stomach. "She hasn't stopped kicking all day."

Laura studied the soccer game in progress. "Then she'll fit in with all her cousins."

Jennifer chuckled. Lexi was running wildly across the grass, beating some of the boys.

"Do you think she's going to make an appearance soon?" Elizabeth asked.

"That's my plan. I haven't consulted her." Jennifer crossed her ankles. "I just have to be mobile by the twentieth."

That was the day of Laura's court appearance. "You don't mean—"

"I mean nothing's keeping us away that day. So this one needs to either hurry up or wait it out. Because I'm going to be there even if I'm in labor."

Laura blinked away the start of tears. "But I don't expect—"

Jennifer crossed her swollen ankles. "You're family, Laura."

Family. She had searched for it all her life. Now one had come to her.

The days were ticking away. On one hand, Laura couldn't wait for the court date. On the other, she wanted to delay it in case the worst happened.

Edward had actually accompanied Gregg and

Paul on their fishing trip. She had been sure
Meredith would put her foot down. But her father-
in-law didn't mention her, just enjoyed the day.

Laura tried to throw herself into her work. Even
though she still loved it, nothing could distract her.

But her friends were determined to try. They
ambushed her at the office one day. From the look
on Paul's face, Laura was pretty sure he'd known
about their plan.

"We're here to kidnap you," Annie announced.

"No point in resisting," Grace told her in her soft-
spoken way.

"We're going for facials and pedicures," Annie
informed her.

Katherine held up a box of Godiva chocolates. "I
brought refreshments."

"Cindy and Emma are meeting us there," Leah
added.

"But I should be working—"

Annie shook her head. "We already checked with
the boss. You're cleared for takeoff."

She didn't feel very festive, but she didn't want
to seem ungrateful, either. When they reached the
salon, the ladies had one more surprise.

Donna stood inside.

Incredibly touched, Laura hugged her best friend.
"What are you doing here?"

"Surprising you. With the help of all your friends."

The grins seemed contagious, touching each face in the semicircle of women.

"I don't know what to say."

Annie's grin broadened. "The toughest decision today is what color nail polish you want."

Katherine waggled her box of Godivas. "And whether you like light or dark chocolate."

She sniffled. "Light. Definitely light."

Chapter Nineteen

"Mom? Guess what?" Kirsten was bubbling over as she rushed into the kitchen. "Mandy's getting better!"

"Oh, sweetie, that's wonderful!" Laura dropped the spoon she was holding to hug her daughter.

"The doctor told her parents that she still has to have a bunch of treatments, but her white cell count is way better."

Laura's eyelids squeezed shut as she imagined the relief Mandy's parents must be feeling. "That's terrific."

"Can Mandy stay over Friday night?"

Since Donna had insisted on staying at the bed-and-breakfast, there wasn't a conflict. "If her parents say it's okay…. Pizza and videos?"

"Could we?"

"News like this deserves a celebration."

Kirsten hugged her again. "Mom?"

"Yes?"

"Oh…nothing…just thinking."

Laura picked up the spoon. "You want to share?"

"Oh, about praying and stuff."

"Your prayers for Mandy?"

"I was kinda thinking about Paul." Kirsten climbed on one of the bar stools. "You know, the devotional. And…you. You said prayers for her every day."

"Her parents would have done the same for us. I knew exactly how they felt." Laura paused as she stirred the batter. "The fear of losing their child. Nothing's worse."

"Do you really feel that way?"

"Why?"

Kirsten made circles on the counter with her fingers. "How come everything's so weird now?"

Laura wished she had the answer. "So many people love you—me, Nana and Grandpa—it's overwhelming at times, isn't it?"

"Do you want to move back to Houston?"

Laura thought of what she had left behind, the new life they had begun to build here. "No, sweetie. I think we're in the right place."

"Nana says you want to keep us from her."

"She's lonely, Kirsten. Losing your dad was harder on her than she wants to let on. Now I guess she's afraid of losing you and Gregg, too. I don't want that for her or for you guys. I don't know what I would have done if I hadn't had my grandmother in my life."

Kirsten hooked her feet on the bottom rung of the stool. "She says you want Paul to take Daddy's place."

"It doesn't work that way. If I find someone else…well, that man would be his own person, not your daddy. Your dad will be with you in your heart and your memories always, no matter what."

Gregg banged open the front door.

"Are we okay, Kirsten?" Laura asked before her son could interrupt them.

"Yeah." Kirsten picked at the cookie dough Laura had been mixing.

Laura wasn't so certain. But Kirsten headed upstairs to do her homework. And Laura knew her child had to think this out on her own.

The morning of the twentieth, Laura awoke so early it was still dark outside. She had only slept in fitful patches through the night. She'd dreamed that the judge had ordered her locked away. Struggling with her fear, she ate a quiet breakfast with the kids.

Paul arrived, dressed in a somber business suit, to drive them to the county courthouse. They were all silent as they climbed the stairs past the lovely old fountain. They located the courtroom and her attorney, Mark Brough, who sat at the defense table.

Her in-laws were sitting with their attorney at the opposing table.

People filed into the chambers and out of the corner of her eye, Laura recognized Paul's parents, his brothers and sisters, even Jennifer. Donna took a seat right behind the defense table. Within minutes Annie and Ethan joined her. Then Grace and Leah. And soon Cindy, Katherine and Emma. Braced by their support, Laura met Paul's eyes and saw his silent encouragement.

They were first on the calendar. After the judge took the bench, Laura listened as the Mannings' attorney laid out the plaintiffs' case. Then her attorney stood and delivered his opening statement. Although she heard every word, Laura knew it wouldn't be the attorneys who decided the case. The judge would hear from the children. And Kirsten was old enough for the judge to weigh her wishes.

Meredith's testimony was tearful as she described her late son and his aspirations for the children. Laura nearly choked. Jerry's aspirations had consisted of escaping to the golf course or barricading himself in his study to avoid the kids. Meredith went on to say she and Edward could provide a more stable environment with both of them to raise the children, that unlike Laura, she didn't have an outside job.

Edward didn't take the stand, instead having chosen to depose his statement.

The judge had already read the depositions from all the character witnesses and called Gregg to his chambers. Even though Gregg was too young to have a legal say in where he wanted to live, the judge wanted to talk to him, get his insight.

While they were gone, Laura gripped the edge of the table. Paul put his hand over hers, rubbing her tightly clenched fingers until she relaxed. Laura's throat was so raw with emotion, she wasn't certain she could speak when it was her turn. And she worried about her little boy, alone in a scary situation. But Gregg had the usual bounce in his step when he emerged from the judge's chambers. And he gave Laura a discreet thumbs-up before he sat down. Paul squeezed her hand. And the clerk called her name.

After she was sworn in, Laura sat stiffly in the witness chair.

Her attorney eased her into her testimony. She explained why she had moved to Rosewood, how she was preparing for a real estate investment career that would insure the children were always well provided for. "My job allows me to be home with the children before and immediately after school. The children are never on their own." She went on to explain that she had developed a network of friends in Rosewood who could help her care for the children if needed.

The opposing attorney attacked this vulnerability. "Isn't it true that on numerous occasions these *friends* have been responsible for the children while your work takes you out of town?"

Laura refused to let him see her tremble. "Yes, but my work has only taken me an hour away from home. And never overnight."

The attorney glanced pointedly at Paul. "Never?"

Her lips thinned as she choked back her anger. "Never."

As her testimony ended and she climbed down from the witness stand, Laura's legs shook. She had done her best, but it all hinged on Kirsten. What would she say?

Kirsten had combed her hair back. She looked so young. Laura caught her breath. For all her grown-up airs, she was too young to have been put in this position.

The judge did the questioning, speaking directly to Kirsten. "You've heard a lot of testimony today, Kirsten. Can you tell me how you feel about living with your mother?"

Laura leaned forward, absently feeling the pressure of Paul's hand on hers.

"I like it," Kirsten answered in a small voice.

"And how do you get on with your grandparents?"

She looked over at Meredith and Edward, then ducked her head. "Good."

The judge glanced at the opposing parties, then

back at Kirsten. "Do you feel your mother neglects you?"

Laura sat paralyzed in the silence of the courtroom.

Then Kirsten met her gaze. "No. My mom's always there for us."

Meredith audibly drew in her breath.

The judge ignored her, concentrating on Kirsten. "Who do you want to live with, Kirsten?"

Kirsten looked at her grandparents, then at Laura. She swallowed. "My mom."

Meredith gasped and Edward took her hand. Their attorney spoke, but Laura didn't hear what he said. After both attorneys had their say, the judge pushed his glasses down on his nose. "Normally I would take the case under advisement, but I feel confident of the facts, and I'm ready to render my decision."

Laura held her breath.

"Custody remains with the defendant, Laura Manning."

The Mannings' attorney stated his intention to appeal.

Voices rose as the judge declared a recess until the next case, then lowered his gavel. As he exited, the courtroom erupted. Laura felt Paul's arms around her in a tight hug. Then she reached for Kirsten and Gregg. It felt as if she'd hugged a hundred people by the time she finally glanced over at Meredith and Edward.

Her mother-in-law was weeping. Edward looked helpless as he tried to support her. And she knew nothing about this victory was sweet.

Chapter Twenty

"Could we take some of these over to Nana and Grandpa's?" Kirsten asked, filching another freshly baked cookie.

Laura glanced at the clock. "It's a school night and you have homework to do."

"It won't take long."

"I don't know." Laura washed her hands. "You usually want to stay there for a while and you need to be in early."

Kirsten took a bite of the cookie. "I want you to go with me."

"I'm not sure that's such a good idea," Laura hedged. She had made it a point not to go there un-invited.

"Please?"

Laura weakened. "Real quick?"

"I promise."

Her mother-in-law was surprised by their unexpected visit. She looked older, Laura realized. Just in the short time since the custody outcome.

Kirsten extended the plate of cookies. "We made these."

Meredith accepted them. "Thank you."

"Mom did most of the work," Kirsten said. "I just put some on the baking sheet."

"I'm sure we'll enjoy them." Meredith said.

"Nana, I need to talk to you and Grandpa."

Meredith frowned. "He's in the living room."

Edward gave them each a hug. Not knowing what her daughter was up to, Laura tentatively took a seat in the chair closest to the door.

"I was just telling Meredith how much I enjoyed my fishing trip with Gregg and Paul," Edward said.

"Gregg did, too," Laura assured him.

Kirsten sat beside Meredith. "Nana, why did you do the court thing about Gregg and me?"

"Because we love you, of course."

Kirsten looked at both her grandparents. "Don't you think my mom loves us?"

"Of course she does," Edward replied.

"Then why did you want to take us away from her?"

Meredith reached for a tissue. "We just want what's best for you."

"Wouldn't that be what we want?" Kirsten fixed her blue eyes, so like her father's, on Meredith.

Edward glanced at his wife. "Yes, it would."

Meredith paled. "What are you saying, Kirsten?"

"I want you to stop the appeal thing."

Meredith's breathing became rapid, shallow. But tears swam in her eyes as she stared at Laura and whispered, "This is your doing."

Laura shook her head.

"Nana, please. It wasn't Mom's idea to come here tonight. It was mine. I just want everybody to like everybody, like Paul's family does."

"It's clear, Laura, that you're trying to replace us with the Russells." Meredith's voice grew stronger as she spoke. "You want to slide Paul into Jerry's place as though he never existed. And his parents as Kirsten and Gregg's grandparents."

Laura felt her pain. "No matter who I might have in my life, you'll always be their grandparents. That won't change. They love you and, more important, I know you love them. Why would I want to deprive my children of something as important as that?"

Meredith bent her head. "I suppose you'd all be happy if we just left."

Kirsten leaned close. "No, Nana. I just want things to be like before. Can't we do that?"

Laura waited for her mother-in-law's reply, wondering if the other woman was capable of bending that much.

"I don't know."

"Please?" Kirsten implored. "Mom says Daddy will be in our hearts forever."

Something flickered in the older woman's eyes. "You did?"

Laura nodded.

"Well, I can't fight all of you," she said finally.

Edward moved to the couch beside his wife and clasped her hand. "We'll drop the appeal."

Kirsten hugged first her grandparents, then ran to Laura.

"I love you, sweetheart."

"Me, too."

"I don't suppose there's much point in our staying in Rosewood," Meredith murmured.

Laura looked over her daughter's head. "Of course there is. The kids are here. And we want you to be part of our lives. That won't ever change."

"There's not that much for us to do here during the week when the kids are in school," Edward mused. "Weekends are different."

"Do you miss Houston?" Laura guessed.

He nodded. "Had my golf foursome. All of us retired. And Meredith had her friends, too. She was busy every day."

Laura looked at her mother-in-law, but didn't voice the question. Where they chose to live would have to be their decision. It was enough to know that she was keeping her children, that the Mannings wouldn't continue the fight. Meredith and Edward weren't as warm as the Russells, but they were family. And she was learning to embrace them all.

Paul was waiting for her when she arrived home. While Kirsten and Gregg had cookies and milk in the kitchen, Laura walked with him in the backyard. "I think I'm still in shock."

Paul looked as happy as she felt. "Kirsten's really proved herself, hasn't she?"

"I had no idea what she planned…. I was so proud of her." Laura took a deep breath. "By the time we left, Meredith and Edward were talking about keeping their house here for weekends and spending the rest of their time in Houston."

"How do you feel about that?"

"If you'd asked me that a few months ago, I'd have been horrified that they were going to spend any time here. But I've been trying to take your mother's advice—looking at Meredith as a person instead of a mother-in-law—and it's helped. She not only lost Jerry, she's been terrified she would lose Kirsten and Gregg, too. I don't want to do that to her. It'll take time, but I think we can come to a better place now that we're not a threat to each other."

"Warm and fuzzy?"

Laura smiled. "She's not like your mother. But she loves the kids."

"So, does this mean you're staying in Rosewood?"

"I still have an internship to complete."

His eyes were searching. "And then?"

"I'm where I want to be."

He clasped her by the arms. "Are you?"

She wanted to tell him just how much. "Yes."

He stepped a fraction closer. "Think you'd consider staying forever?"

Trembling, she stroked his cheek. "Forever?"

"I love you, Laura."

She couldn't stop the tears that blurred her vision. "Tears?"

"I love you, too," she managed. "I just can't believe you…feel the same."

He threaded his fingers through her hair. "Don't you know how remarkable you are? I've waited all my life for you. I want us to be a family, you, me, Kirsten, Gregg."

Family and love? Laura wanted to shout to the skies. Instead her voice was a whisper, a promise. "Yes. Oh, yes."

His lips were gentle against hers, also a promise.

"I don't ever want you to be hurt again," he vowed. "And I plan to make sure you aren't."

Her heart quaked, knowing it was a vow that would take them into that forever.

Epilogue

Cream-colored roses tied with a silk ribbon matched both the color and simplicity of Laura's vintage dress. She stared into the full-length mirror. It was real. The dress, the flowers, the ceremony that was about to take place.

An emerald-cut diamond sparkled on her left hand. Paul had placed it there soon after she had agreed to marry him. Laura had been nervous about telling her in-laws. She and Paul had gone together to give them the news, and he had assured the Mannings that he wanted them to be part of his family. Meredith had wavered, looking so sad that Laura had embraced her. Instead of pulling away, Meredith admitted she wanted to be included. So Laura had asked her to be in charge of the catering for the reception.

Elizabeth stuck her head into the bride's room. "May I come in?"

"Please. I'm just pinching myself to make sure this is real."

Elizabeth stepped inside. "That's how I felt on my wedding day, too. Oh my…you're so beautiful."

"Paul makes me feel that way."

Elizabeth smoothed a wisp of Laura's hair that fell across her forehead. "Do you have something borrowed to wear?"

"Donna went to find something—a hankie, I think. The dress is old." She touched the pearl and flower coronet on her head. "This is new and Jennifer gave me a blue garter."

Elizabeth held up a simple strand of pearls. "I wore these on my wedding day. My mother did, too. And my girls. It's a family tradition. I was hoping that, as my newest daughter, you would, too."

Touched beyond measure, Laura fought against tears.

"Now we can't have you ruining your makeup," Elizabeth chided gently, using her own handkerchief to dry Laura's eyes. "My girls always look special walking down the aisle."

Her girls. Laura had never heard anything sweeter.

"I'd better go and check on Kirsten and Gregg. They're practicing their parts." Elizabeth hugged her close, then left again.

Kirsten was Laura's only bridesmaid. And Paul had chosen Gregg for his best man.

Donna darted inside. "I think it's time."

Laura took one last look in the mirror. "I'm ready."

Music filled the sanctuary, swelling as the organist played the age-old wedding song. Kirsten and Gregg walked Laura up the aisle, prepared to give her to the man who would also love and nurture them.

When it was time, Paul took her hand and slipped a gold band on her finger. It looked so right. Her hand shook as she placed the matching band on his finger.

Taking each vow, Laura pledged herself to this man, this marriage.

"I now pronounce you husband and wife."

Turning to the congregation, Laura looked out at everyone who had become dear to her.

Better than a dream. Hand in hand, they walked back down the aisle as the guests stood to watch them.

Paul lifted her hand to his lips. "You're mine now, Laura Russell."

"And you, mine. I'm not dreaming, am I?"

"You are a vision."

"Promise me something?"

"Anything."

"Don't ever change."

"That's one promise I can't make." He eased his thumb over her cheek. "Because every day I'm going to love you more."

That was a change she could live with.

People gathered around them, offering their congratulations. They moved slowly toward the reception, which was being held in the adjacent hall.

Meredith buzzed around the room, checking on the caterers. The tables were exquisitely dressed, the food impeccable. She had done a beautiful job.

Each of Paul's siblings came through the line to officially welcome Laura into the family. No empty gestures, they gave her big hugs and wide smiles.

Charles's eyes were suspiciously moist as he greeted her. "I knew Paul would find the perfect woman. It's a tradition with the men in our family."

What a dear man. "I'm the lucky one—he'll be the perfect husband."

He kissed her cheek. "And that's why you two will always be happy."

At the end of the line, Laura spotted Edward and Meredith. He offered a hug and congratulations. Meredith didn't speak for a moment. Then she held out her hand. "Congratulations."

Laura chose to hug her instead. "Thank you, Meredith. For everything."

"Everyone's raving about the food," Paul added. "Thank you."

Meredith looked pleased. "No trouble."

But it had been. The good kind. Like her offer to have the children stay with them during the honeymoon.

"You know how much I like our friends and

family," Paul said later when the guests began to concentrate on the buffet rather than the bride and groom.

She smiled.

"And that I think you did a fantastic job planning the wedding…"

"Umm."

"But do I ever get to be alone with my bride?"

She felt her heart beat faster. "I'm guessing you'll have about fifty years to do that."

"Only fifty? I'm thinking at least seventy-five."

"Promise?"

"For you…anything. And everything."

But she already had it. A fantastic husband, her faith, loyal friends and the family she'd always dreamed of.

She met his kiss, feeling the tenderness of his lips, the depth of his heart. And knew what it was to love again.

* * * * *

Dear Reader,

I've always believed in second chances, new beginnings. I'm not sure where my life would be without them. For Laura Manning, it's a matter of survival. Often the scars of past relationships blight our attempts at a new start, our very sense of hope itself. Friends, fellowship and love can revive the most wounded spirit, especially in Rosewood. It's a town that embraces the best in all of us—encourages our hope and most especially our faith.

It's my hope that you'll enjoy another sojourn to a place we can all call our own.

God Bless,

Bonnie K. Winn

QUESTIONS FOR DISCUSSION

1. Would you have liked to have seen the Mannings return to Houston to keep the family together? Why or why not?

2. Was Laura justified in pulling up roots and resettling in Rosewood? Why do you think so (or not)? Could she have been happy staying in Houston?

3. Do you agree with Paul's ex-girlfriend, that his single-minded devotion to his family makes him a less admirable hero—with little time to give to a significant other?

4. Did you believe in Paul's mother's ready acceptance of Laura? Why or why not?

5. Was Paul's reluctance to think badly of his late friend a good or bad trait? Explain.

6. What effect would Laura's faith have had on her choice to marry Jerry if it had been strong?

7. Do you believe Laura's first marriage would've been worse if her husband had abused her physically rather than emotionally?

8. Put yourself in Laura's shoes. If Kirsten had chosen to live with her grandparents over her mother, what would you have done?

9. What better reward could Laura have had than becoming part of the Russell family?

10. Did you feel the Manning grandparents were treated fairly? How would you have treated them?

Love Inspired®
SUSPENSE
RIVETING INSPIRATIONAL ROMANCE

Watch for our new series of
edge-of-your-seat suspense novels.
These contemporary tales
of intrigue and romance
feature Christian characters
facing challenges to their faith...
and their lives!

**NOW AVAILABLE IN REGULAR
AND LARGER-PRINT FORMATS.**

Steple
Hill®

Visit:
www.steeplehillbooks.com

LISUSDIR07

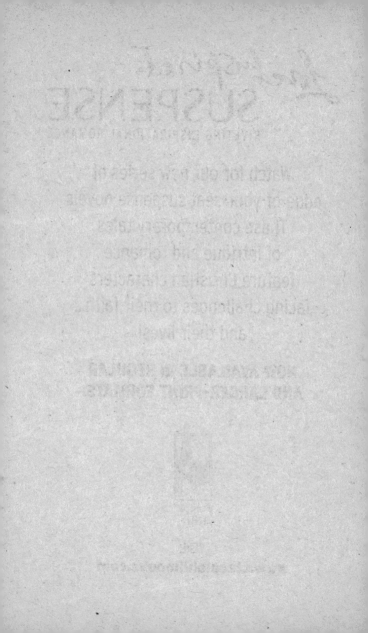